"Sara Levine's sardonic amusements engage and horrify. This is comedy as guillotine. If you are brave you may want to put your head in it."—JESSE BALL

"Here I must confess an error. Back in August, I listed this book as a memoir…I mistook the time-honored fiction-in-the-voice-of-a-quirky-narrator as the real thing. In fact, Levine…has crafted a sassy first novel about a woman needing a life fix who hooks onto Robert Louis Stevenson's *Treasure Island* as her salvation. After all, there's so much to learn from hero Jim Hawkins: courage, resolution…and horn-blowing. Clearly, among other things, this rather spoofs the whole heal-myself memoir genre—and I got taken. I really do like this better as fiction, and since Alice Sebold liked it, too, selecting it for publication, you can't go wrong."—BARBARA HOFFERT, Prepub Alert (*Library Journal*)

"When someone spikes your rum cocktail you want it to have the punch and the smooth finish that this novel does. Levine is simultaneously politically incorrect yet humane in this wild romp of a modern farce. Avast ye people, open up and let the Levine shine in!"—ALICE SEBOLD

"…pray tell me *yes! Treasure Island!!!* deserves every one of its exclamation marks."—JIM KRUSOE

"Slightly deranged and marvelous."—MARCY DERMANSKY

"In this brilliant star of a book, a new kind of anti-hero is off on her self-destructive quest, full of rotten ideas and bad choices. She begs us, *dares us*, not to like her—but we do. Oh yes, we certainly do. Addictive reading. Hilarious. Lively. Necessary. Bravo!"—DEB OLIN UNFERTH

"*Treasure Island!!!* is outrageous, surprising, frightening, and funny, funny, funny—a hip grandchild of Poe, Nabokov and Peanuts' Lucy Van Pelt."—MARK O'DONNELL

TREASURE ISLAND!!!

Sara Levine

TREASURE ISLAND!!!

Europa
editions

Europa Editions
214 West 29th Street
New York, N.Y. 10001
www.europaeditions.com
info@europaeditions.com

Library of Congress Cataloging in Publication Data is available
ISBN 978-1-60945-061-8

Levine, Sara
Treasure Island!!!

Book design by Emanuele Ragnisco
www.mekkanografici.com

Cover illustration by Marina Sagona

Prepress by Grafica Punto Print – Rome

Printed in the USA

for Stephen, Lillian and Marty

With your faults, don't hurry.
Don't correct them thoughtlessly.
What would you put in their place?
—HENRI MICHAUX

TREASURE ISLAND!!!

I n the aftermath of my adventure, I decided to write down the whole thing, starting with my discovery of *Treasure Island* and keeping nothing back, not even the names of the friends and family members whose problems plagued me; and so even though I'd *love* to go into the other room and stab someone with a kitchen knife, I take up my pen—a nifty micro-ball which had been incorrectly capped and would have dried out had I not, at the crucial moment, found it and restored its seal.

The Pen

Before I Put My Hand To It   *After* a Good Shake, A Lick of
                                       the Nib, and Recapping

Though even with pencil, I could tell this story pretty well.

My sister said it was an adventure book and that the trouble with adventure books was "all action and no feeling." She said that the book had the moral complexity of a baseball game and that her hand would force no nine-year-old girl to read it.

She said a few more self-righteous, priggish things and then off she went, leaving *Treasure Island* on my futon, along with *Palomino Pal* and *Ride on the Unicorn's Back*, though what was wrong with those books—I mean, according to her—I don't know. For a third-grade teacher my sister is pretty careless. Later she called and said, "Would you return the books I left at your place to the library?"

"Why didn't you like this one called *Treasure Island*?" I said.

"Don't tell me you're reading it," Adrianna said. "I *hate* a book with no girls in it."

Does such a knee-jerk sensibility deserve to be recorded? But I am writing in a very nice unlined Muji notebook and I can always go back and cross out her insufferable parts later.

"Don't tell me you're reading it," she said, as if I were doing something to the book, whereas in fact the book was doing something to me. I'm twenty-five years old and this happened on a Monday when I didn't have to work at The Pet Library and had no plans except to sleep and maybe wash my bras in the sink, and that was a big maybe. Birds chirped, shadows fell on the linoleum, in the distance a weed trimmer whined. When I got to the part where Long John Silver's gang captures Jim Hawkins in the deserted stockade, Lars, my boyfriend, left a message on my voicemail, saying did I want to go out for a burrito.

Here is my life, I thought.

And *there* is the adventurous life kicking out the covers of Stevenson's novel.

When had I ever dreamed a scheme? When had I ever done a foolish, over-bold act? When had I ever, like Jim Hawkins, broke from my friends, raced for the beach, stolen a boat, killed a man, or eliminated an obstacle that stood in the way of my getting a hunk of gold? I, a person unable to decide what to do with my broken mini-blinds, let alone with the rest of my life, lay on my bed, while in the book's open air, people chased assholes out of pubs and trampled blind beggars with their horses. You needn't have a violent nature to be impressed with animal energy. If life were a sea adventure, I knew: I wouldn't be sailor, pirate, or cabin boy but more likely a barnacle clinging to the side of the boat. Why not rise, I thought. Why not spring up that very moment, in the spirit of Jim, and create my own adventure?

"That's how I felt when I saw *He's Just Not That Into You* on Oprah," Rena said. "That book explained everything, everything, about me and Dougie Thomas."

Personally, I think the fact that he called himself 'Dougie' explained everything about Rena and Dougie Thomas. That and the fact that they'd met at a Christmas caroling party he single-handedly organized; but I never tell friends their boyfriends are probably gay, so I let the matter drop. Rena is a close friend; she knows firsthand my history of low-paying jobs and hapless boyfriends. This was the following day, when she and I were sitting in our favorite coffee shop eating Gratuitous Pancakes, her name for the meal taken when she has recently eaten lunch and I have recently woken up. That day, I'd slept late only because I'd been up all night finishing *Treasure Island*, and I was thrilled to tell Rena my discovery. But as we talked, I felt I was leading a clumsy tourist through the jungle of my thoughts.

Rena lagged, slapped at mosquitoes, tripped on roots, missed the waterfall. A painful truth I'd learn later: you may be ready to grow, but you can't fertilize friends and grow them with you. I must have been the tiniest of boats rocking on the sea of Robert Louis Stevenson's consciousness, I told Rena; I must have been a sea-bird streaking through the azure sky of his daydream; in just the same way spirits are said to commune across cultures, time, and continents, Robert Louis Stevenson's book *Treasure Island* felt *cosmically intended* for me.

"Isn't it a kids' book?" Rena said.

"That doesn't matter. It's sophisticated. It has multiple levels. A lot of the vocabulary I had to look up."

"And isn't it a boys' book?" Rena said.

Okay maybe, but so what? When I was in fourth grade I kept a large, profusely illustrated chart to show all the books I read, and I remember now that the books were pretty girly. I did piles of Judy Blume, beams of Beverly Cleary. When the librarian pushed, I did *Anne of Green Gables*. Then I discovered jump rope and drifted toward the playground faction with the best rhymes. "All in together, girls. How do you like the weather, girls?" Then came sticker collecting. Then friendship pins. I believe I lost a whole year of school to their assembly. When we were supposed to be following the presidential election on TV, I was studying Jenny Galassi's sneakers and trying to figure out how she had gotten more friendship pins than me. In fifth grade, the year we did the continents, my mother confronted me with my warped cardboard reading chart. "Is this important?" she said. "I found it behind the radiator." Maybe a boys' book was exactly what I needed. And it was a classic; gold letters said so right on the cover.

"This book is going to change my life."

But it's useless to explain the prospect of personal change. Thousands of dollars in student loans to major in philosophy, and now she unlocked apartments every day in order to meet the superficial needs of half-crazed animals. Rena Deutsch, Freelance Pet Sitter. She wasn't stupid, but there she was, covered in cat hair. Compared to her, I was highly evolved.

"Rena, I'm so serious about this, it hurts. What has the hero of *Treasure Island* got that I haven't got? How can I become a hero of my own life?"

"You're tired of your job at the Library. Maybe you should go back to school. Get a master's degree in something. You were always good at writing papers."

I felt a tiny jolt of pleasure. But I knew it wasn't true. Rena and I had gone to a state university, where many of the courses culminated in a machine-read Scantron test, the kind of test that measures knowledge with no compassion for error. The iron quality of the directions alone had filled me with dread: "Do not make any stray marks on the answer sheet," "Fill in each circle completely," "To change your answer completely erase the mark." After racking up a row of D's and F's my freshman year, I avoided any class that required a Scantron and somehow wound up as an English major. Thus Rena remembered me writing lots of little pastorals, in which a simple-minded thesis shepherded its wooly flock of evidence over hills and dales and *very* shallow rivers. English majors never failed; at worst, their opinions simply differed from their teachers', and everyone agreed that this difference could be adequately expressed with a C and a down-tilting minus. But I ask you reader, where had all that paper writing got me? *Fill in the circle completely:*

O Nowhere!

So I shrugged off Rena's compliment and delved into my backpack for the golden compass I had made for my new life. This was not a long, gangly composition; I had merely— merely!—written down boy hero Jim Hawkins' best qualities, which formed, I realized every moment with increasing warmth, the Core Values of Robert Louis Stevenson's *Treasure Island*.

I am copying it out hurriedly here; of course, the original was carefully hand-lettered in a serifed style on a creamy seventy-pound piece of paper with a lovely deckled edge.

BOLDNESS
RESOLUTION
INDEPENDENCE
HORN-BLOWING

Rena put her hand on my arm gently, as if expecting to get burned. "Are you taking your Zoloft?" she said.

CHAPTER 2

Treasure Island—as you have ample reason to know, having read it yourself or heard about it or seen the movie or maybe eaten in the restaurant Long John Silver's—is a classic of boys' adventure fiction, and almost immediately was recognized as a masterpiece when it was published in 1883. The funny thing is—and it took me ages to even remember this—I first read the book, or a portion of it, when it was over a hundred years old and I was nine. Mrs. Buskirk had assigned the first few chapters to our fifth grade Reading Lab. Dimly I recall the sensation of sitting at a kidney-shaped table and reading a paragraph out loud; in fact, it was the part where Billy Bones shows up at the inn where Jim is living a quiet life with his parents: *"This is a handy cove and a pleasant sittyated grog-shop . . . Here you, matey, bring up alongside and help up my chest . . . What you mought call me? You mought call me captain."* Obviously I bumped my shins against a few phrases like these and decided the book was too alien to interest. I don't blame me. Book aside, by the end of that Reading Lab, I do remember being keyed up and excited. Not because of Jim Hawkins, but because we girls sat with our hands below desk level, passing around Patty Pacholewski's bracelets and rings. She had *amazing* jewelry.

At age twenty-five, you can't read a rip-roaring book like *Treasure Island* and not feel adventure tug on your hand, even if your hand is firmly planted in your pocket, fingering a pigment-dense tube of lip gloss. You waken to the possibilities of bravery and you chafe a good deal at that thing other people call security. (My mother happened to call it health insurance, a 401(k), and opportunity for advancement. My stay-at-home mom!) But Rena was right; for a long time I'd been dissatisfied with my job, even though The Pet Library was a better gig than the things I'd done before: part-time office assistant at an insurance company; full time scooper at Pignut Ice Cream . . . I could but won't go on.

The Pet Library job had fallen into my lap—six months before this story properly begins—when a friend of a friend of my mother's, having heard I was looking for meaningful work, sent along the phone number of a "lady seeking an assistant." I was to meet Ms. Wang at The Donut Hole and, after scanning the tables for the Chinese-American equivalent of my matronly mother, I discovered an angular woman in her forties, wearing a sweater dress with a shawl collar and (I need make no secret of it now) gladiator-style wedge boots that would have looked just as right on me. She quickly dismissed my work experience and asked me soul-searching questions along the lines of "what is your principles? What is your values in life?" The more indistinct my answers were, the more she liked them, and after two apple fritters and a large quantity of coffee, her manner gave every indication that the meeting had been a success. "You come to Pet Library?" she said, and I answered, "Sure."

A week later, on an unseasonably cold day, I pushed open the glass door to a smell so high that, had I come by car, I would have turned back immediately; but knowing the next bus wouldn't come for an hour, I felt bound to carry through. I remember thinking, I hope Ms. Wang won't mind that I'm dressed casually—and then, having heard the door chime, a figure flung itself out of the back room, enveloped in a hideous, ankle-length smock of waxed cotton. She took my hands; the intimacy was mildly thrilling. Soon I was trailing her around, asking breathless questions about the collection's history. She seemed grateful for my questions; the acquisition of a tree squirrel swelled, plot-wise, into a triple-decker Victorian sensation novel: "Wow," I kept saying. "You're kidding! No! And then what?" I can't account for it, but before the hour was over, I'd signed on to do four shifts a week.

She didn't ask me to wear a waxed smock and I had limited contact with humans: I soon learned that pretty much covered the perks. Nancy Wang had created The Pet Library in a strip mall out of her own scrappy savings and seemed to think that she had paid her dues by whatever she had suffered in China. The level of passion she expected from me about menial duties I doubt I could have mustered even if I'd been raised by a low-born family in Beijing. One day, just after dipping into Chapter XXII: How My Sea Adventure Began, I was trimming the rabbits' nails and thinking how if Jim Hawkins got himself into a stupid job, he would find a way to wriggle out of it. Jim was always dashing away, sheering off, giving someone the slip. A model of boyish energy! Meanwhile here I was, cravenly struggling with grunting mammals. One particularly solid rabbit, a Flemish Giant named Bobby, kept squirming out of the towel and scratching my forearms. Finally, rather than continue the task, I took him up by the ears and pitched him back into the cage, three paws untrimmed. A little later Nancy, who had been massaging Willie the poodle's lower gum line, looked into the hutch and remarked, "Bobby needs his nails finished," to which I replied, "Bobby needs a lot of things that he won't be getting as well." There followed a battle of looks that ended, I am happy to say, with Nancy taking up Bobby herself for trimming. I stood resolute and refused to hold even his legs. *Hello, backbone*, I muttered as I walked away.

It was intoxicating to realize I could say no to her. A few days later when she asked, "Did you clean litter boxes?" I said,

"By god I did not clean the litter boxes." The truth is I *had* cleaned them but I was still getting the hang of the "no" business and liked the way the word felt in my mouth. Eventually I got better at asserting myself and she began to chide me regularly. "You read book," she would say. "Time to feed hamsters. Later you read book!" One afternoon I was sitting at the desk—with Jim Hawkins just about to tear open Billy Bones' shirt—when Nancy playfully tipped the book shut.

"What are you doing?" I said coldly.

I forget now exactly what she wanted, but she repeated the demands without pausing for breath and claimed that whenever she turned around, I wasn't working: "Floor dirty, you read book! Animal hungry, you read book!" Yes, I said, "I read book."

I'd drop my book for an emergency, but to remedy the slowly accreting smell of urine in a room dedicated to the accrual of urine, I didn't know. Maybe she didn't know the word "accretion," but she definitely took my tone.

I was pretty pleased with how that encounter ended, but when I told Lars, he expressed alarm. Lars was a mild-mannered guy and worried a good deal about offending people. His own boss happened to be a boisterous, supportive teddy bear of a guy, which inclined Lars to see employers as somewhat sympathetic and endearing—and this no matter how often I told him about Nancy's flaws. I think he was too invested in my image as a nice girl (docile, accommodating) to appreciate the emotional territory I was exploring. Was I a bit acerbic at times? Yes, I was—not just with Nancy, but with him. I heard Lars out, of course, but in the end I dismissed his worries. It's what Dr. Livesey would have done.

As I grew more confident about what BOLDNESS meant, I began to see that the real problem was I had been letting Nancy define my job for me. She was my boss, of course, but from the moment I had been hired, my duties—which as far as

I was concerned were somewhat flexible—had devolved to drudgery of the most degrading sort. When I think about all the different things I might have done for The Pet Library— well, it almost seems a joke! I could have been entrusted with budget, or community outreach, or acquisitions—not that I was terribly interested in any of these things—but instead Nancy had me scraping out litter boxes. I never said this out loud, but also I objected to the fact that she made no effort to build a more varied collection of animals. Before my time, she'd set up a super-size drop-off kennel in the parking lot for discards and, if anything, the Library had become the town's dumping ground for unwanted cats and dogs. Two weeks after Easter, you should have seen the rabbit landslide. Certainly I'm no economist, but even I could tell that the llamas, who stayed in a three-sided shelter out back, wouldn't qualify as a cost-effective acquisition. The enormous amount of care they required—which Nancy claimed stemmed from their emo-tional problems (they'd been abandoned by their previous owners after a bitter divorce)—hardly balanced out the minor delight they afforded patrons. No one had the *space* to check them out, although people at the Shop 'n' Go sometimes stared at the llamas' scabs as they loaded their groceries. Why didn't she put *me*, a college graduate, in charge of acquisitions?

It's dumbfounding, but even after I'd read *Treasure Island* a few times, I clung to my bitterness and didn't do all that much to change my situation. For a while my attitude was: "I don't mind sitting up here at the counter, reading my book, and charging out a cat or two, but I am *not* going to fall all over myself checking the hermit crabs' bedding for fungus gnats." I told myself I was a circulation librarian, not a cleaning service, and I consoled myself with small liberties—being slow to feed the fish, for example (*they* can't complain), or dipping into Nancy's Post-its supply and taking notes on Chapter XXV: I Strike the Jolly Roger.

"But you have to be careful," Lars said when we talked about it over burritos. "If you lost your job, what would you do? Unless you want to borrow money again from your parents."

I didn't want to get into a money discussion with Lars. I was pretty sure he had more of it, though it had taken me a while to catch on since he works a low-paying job at a computer help desk and spends next to *nothing* on his clothes. "How'd you get *that*?" I'd said the first night I stumbled drunkenly into his condo. Turns out that behind even a slightly bedraggled guy there can lurk a Bang & Olufsen sound system. "What kind of music do you like?" he answered and further discussion got muffled in the make-out moves. Since then we had managed to dance around the big ugly sinkhole subject of money. I knew that two years ago he'd backpacked in Guatemala and had immediately paid off his debts for the trip by cleaning a foundry. I suspected he had a work ethic I wasn't interested in exploring.

"*Treasure Island*," Lars mused. "Ever worry that if you only read one book, you'll get scurvy of the brain?"

"You can learn a lot by reading deeply into one book. In fact, in Japan, that's how literature is studied. People read one book all year. It's only the stupid Americans who skitter around."

"*Who* reads one book a year?"

"Japanese literature majors."

He looked skeptical. "I'll ask my friend Yusuke."

"No, don't. We're off the point. Weren't we talking about my lousy job?"

Lars paused to ingest some refried beans. "I'm reading this book about the Beslan school siege. In Russia, remember? When Shamil Basayev sent those jihadists to slaughter school children in North Ossetia?"

"Excuse me?" I muttered. "I'm eating."

"Okay, maybe you wouldn't like it. The situation is *so* fucked up. The violence alone—"

"I don't know what you think *Treasure Island* is, Lars, but people do kick it. Heads roll."

Lars smiled. "*The Federalist Papers*," he went on. "That was the last thing I read. No, no—it's good, but I think you might find it a little dry. You prefer fiction, right? I know: the new Nora Roberts! You ever read Nora Roberts?"

I sighed. "I'm not *looking* for a book, Lars."

"Did you ever think about joining a book club, though? My office mate, Chelsea, does a reading group, and she might have room for another person. They meet at The Flying Saucer. I've seen the books on her desk—history, linguistics, science stuff—it's pretty broad. Chelsea says they read *great* books."

"Great books? Great books? Lars, would you know a great book if it hit you in the ass with its registration papers? *Treasure Island* is a great book!"

I dropped my burrito into its soggy bed of shredded lettuce. Was Lars capable of recognizing *merit*? The lanky brown hair, the smudge on his glasses, the inability to intuit I was too sophisticated for some geeky co-worker's book group. A stray thought wandered into my mind and swished its mangy tail: should I dump him?

"Have you even *read* it yet, Lars?"

"I'm going to."

"Yeah, that's what Rena said, too. But now she's all caught up in some dutiful tome on global warming."

I pulled *Treasure Island* out of my backpack and nudged his plate aside, so that the volume lay before him on the Formica table. Something about the tableau reminded me of the time Aunt Boothie parked me in front of her photo album so I could get the blow-by-blow on the Senior Singles Mississippi Riverboat Tour.

"Okay," I said, "of course, I'm not going to force this down your throat," and refrained from pointing out the passages I deemed most important.

"Are you saying you want me to read it now?" Lars said.

"I'm tempted to read it *aloud* to you, but I don't want to be a control freak."

"No, don't," he said quickly, and we agreed he could wade into the book at his own pace. Which turned out to be deadly slow if not downright chicken-shit. It was a book; what was he afraid of? I ate a basket of chips while he lingered on the frontispiece: a dull brown map of the island, porcupined with lines illustrating I don't know what: longitudes, latitudes. Turn the page, I urged him silently. Turn the page, plunge in!

"I find maps interesting," he said.

So violently did I expel my breath, I spat on the map—one of those weird, nervous spits where you accidentally trigger a salivary gland and, as if your tongue had discovered your mouth's G-spot, the saliva erupts in a concentrated jet. Thinking I'd meant to do it—"gleeking," he called it; as if I'd ever "gleek" on my bible!—he took the occasion of my nervous laughter to close the book. "Let's order two flans," he said affably, and thus our discussion of the salty book was derailed by sugar.

Something has to budge, I thought as we walked home that night, arm in arm, ostensibly happy, but inwardly one of us (me) seething. Already I felt big with book the way a woman feels big with child. Was there room in this relationship for the two of us?

"Lars, I want us to talk *seriously* about *Treasure Island*," I said as we reached my apartment. "Like, pretend we're in a seminar."

"Piracy and the expansion of the nineteenth-century nation-state," he replied. "I'll talk for twenty minutes and then turn it over to you and Jimbo."

"Jim," I said. "Jim Hawkins."

"Whoa, you're mauling the door! Didn't I tell you," Lars said as if this were *his* apartment, "turn the key and pull at the same time. Otherwise it sticks." He put his hand over mine and pulled. The door popped open.

Inside, Lars removed my backpack and slung it on the futon. We kissed, and the kiss was a wrecking ball; walls crumbled, plaster sifted, a grey bird flew through the dust and emerged white as snow. What a heap! Later somebody from the salvage department would come by and look for usable, well-conditioned pieces of me.

"What's a 'nineteenth-century nation-state'?" I asked later as I searched the tangled sheets for my underthings. But Lars had drifted off to sleep.

CHAPTER 3

Cooped up in a library with twelve rabbits, eight hamsters, six hermit crabs, one rooster, four large sullen cats, a tank of fish, five mutts, and a purebred poodle whose needs are as bountiful as the sea, a person gets to thinking. Neither Rena nor Lars was helping to strengthen the hold of *Treasure Island* on my life; they *said* they were supportive, but talking to them about the book's Core Values—

BOLDNESS
RESOLUTION
INDEPENDENCE
HORN-BLOWING

—was about as interesting as talking to a couple of Tic Tacs. What I wanted to bring the message home was a parrot, a parrot who would sit on my shoulder every day, or at least every day I worked at The Pet Library, and be a living, squawking reminder of the active role I meant to play in my life. In *Treasure Island* Long John Silver's parrot shouts, "Pieces of eight! Pieces of eight!" Mine would shout, "Be bold, but be kind, be yourself but be plucky, be flexible and yet tenacious," assuming a parrot could be trained to say such a long and syntactically complex thing. If not, I would accept "Steer the boat, girlfriend!"

The morning I fixed on the idea of the parrot happened to be a morning Nancy had taken her ancient mother to physical therapy and wouldn't be back until noon. The library was awash in gloom. One of the cats had been vomiting and because I'd been pretending not to see the puddles, the place stank. Also, the week before, in a fit of apathy, I had allowed a teenager without any ID to check out the rooster, and now the bird was back, its neck feathers ruffled and a stormy look in its eye. In the old days, by which I mean my pre-*Treasure Island* days, I wouldn't have thought of leaving that smelly Pet Library, I would have soaked up the bad air and all the rest until Nancy came back to release me. Oh yes, I am quite sure, in the old days, my tiny train of thought would have circled around a papier-mâché landscape of imaginary needs and catastrophes, and thinking I was obliged to stay at work, I would have missed an opportunity for decisive action. But I had a scheme in my head.

The point of the scheme was to show Nancy that I was capable of action. Lately, our relations had been tense, and I didn't want to waste any energy discussing the further responsibilities I craved. No, I would *show* her she could rely on me and I knew just the way to do it. As I cast my eye around the dreary room, a dozen ideas for improvement flooded my head.

Nancy, who had an immigrant's mistrust of banks, kept a box of petty cash in the back room. A few times I had seen her open the box before she sent me out, like an errand girl, for feed. Now I removed the key from its hiding place and though the lock was very stiff, I turned it and threw back the lid. A faint smell rose from the interior, almost like scented toilet paper or over-ripe apples, but nothing was on top except a plastic tray containing a few pieces of junk jewelry, a pair of foam earplugs, and a harvest of bright red, floozy-length Lee Press-On Nails. I pulled up the tray with impatience, and there lay ten crisp one hundred dollar bills. Nancy! I'd never dreamed she had this much capital! If only she would trust me with it—and here I lost a few moments to a potent daydream in which I tore out the Library's U-shaped circ desk and installed a slab of black walnut. Or Zebra Wood. Then I shook myself awake and pocketed the cash. I returned the key to its hiding place, and was about to make for the door when I heard a sound that brought my heart into my mouth—the door chime chirp, alerting me that we had a patron. As I came out of the back room, I saw it was a boy come to return a goldfish. He was about ten years old and walked, the little glass loaner bowl close to his chest, as if he had another ten years to make the journey from the door to . . .

"Hurry up then," I said. "You won't drop it. I was about to close up."

Goldfish returns are the easiest, or should be, since you don't have to interact with the pet. When you do a mammal return, you stroke the animal and make a big fuss to pretend you missed it. With the goldfish, I just checked to make sure its fins were still there, and dumped it back into the tank. I didn't even pretend to know which fish it was. "Vinny, huh? Alberto, huh? Or is this Iphigenia?" "This is Percevaux," the boy said. "Sure it is, good old Percevaux." I grabbed the record book, found the boy's name, and crossed it off. (Another way Nancy might have used me better: Hello, computer age!) "You're all clear," I told the boy. He had followed me over to the tank and remained there, watching Percevaux flick a fin. "It's not the circus," I said. "Come on, I'll walk you out." In my haste I forgot to lock the door.

On the pavement the boy threatened to walk my way, but by lingering at the corner and pretending that I was about to catch a bus, I quickly shed him. You have to be careful in this job; certain kids glom on to a Pet Librarian as if to a celebrity. Something of the animal glamour attaches, the way it would for a zookeeper or a lion tamer. I don't pretend to understand it, but fortunately this boy wasn't too hard to shake. "You ever think about maybe getting a panda?" he said dreamily. When I roared, "No!" he scuttled off.

For reasons I don't wish to go into, I don't have a car, and I was too impatient to wait for a bus, so I began to walk. Walk and walk and walk, past pizzerias and dry cleaners and fast lube franchises until I reached Cutwater Mall, a downscale place with a crappy food court and a hideous green and black linoleum floor rolling past stores with names like Gifts 'n' Things and Sox 'n' Stuff. My family used to go here before a better mall was built—one with skylights and a fiberglass reproduction of the Trevi fountain.

The pet shop I wanted sat in a dark corner on the lower level, its floor seething with woodchips and hair. Puppies and kittens cowered in the front window, fish tanks bubbled and glowed along the sides. I threaded my way through the mess and found a regal teenaged girl, her hair done up so elaborately she appeared to wear a Zulu basket on her head. Lethargically she unpacked a crate of ferret shampoo.

"I came for a parrot."

For the benefit of anyone who has never been to a mall pet store, the people who work there don't know a thing about pets, nor would they care to. Without any affect she led me to aisle nine. There, in the fluorescent corridor, after rows of twittering songbirds, none of whom caught my fancy, I discovered a cage labeled "Yellow-Naped Amazon." Its occupant was one foot high and came at my eye like a bit of migraine, its feathers so brightly colored the air around them seemed to pulse. I studied the hard curled beak and two glittering eyes, one of which studied me. Then the bird made an unearthly noise, a metallic call pitched to pierce through hundreds of miles of Amazon canopy.

"I don't know if it's a boy or a girl," the salesgirl told me. "They don't come in tagged. But we call it Richard. Little Richard." Having done her duty, she turned away, and as the sweet perfume of her hair oil receded, a musty smell took precedence in my nostrils. Bird. Bird smell. Did I want to bring this thing into my workplace? It was larger and more alive than

I had expected. Running back and forth along the perch, "Little Richard" let loose a long, harassing whistle.

"I'm a fool, if you like"—I walked the aisles in panic—"and certainly I'm going to do a foolish, over-bold act, but I'm determined to do it"—which is what Jim Hawkins says when he sets out to recapture the ship from the pirates. I found the salesgirl, tapped her on the shoulder.

"You want him?"

I clutched a shelf for balance and accidentally knocked down a noisy Swat 'n' Swing. "I do and I don't, of course. I came for a parrot, but I wonder if a parrot is really the thing. Does he creep *you* out? Look at that tongue, I didn't even realize birds had tongues. You're probably getting minimum wage, and here I am, taking up your time, trying to figure out . . . I *love* your hair, by the way."

She didn't smile; she heard that compliment all the time.

"The thing is, I'm torn. What do you think?"

"Why do you care what *I* think?"

But I did care, I mean not pathologically, but a little. In another scenario, this girl and I might become friends. I looked at the bird and imagined it sitting on my shoulder and pecking my eyes out. The girl turned around to . . . "Wait!" I shrilled. I picked up the cage, produced the cash, and in a loud, jovial voice, announced that I would buy it.

I began to feel pretty excited as I walked the parrot back to The Pet Library. He was excited too. He screamed the whole way.

A car filled with teenage boys came roaring by, its tires spitting mud, and one of the boys stuck out his head and called, "Eeeeeeeeeeeyaaaaaaa Polly, want a cracker?" which was not even *remotely* witty, and yet as witnesses to my bold business, they were somehow kindred; they were scrappy, fearless fellow adventurers. I waved and walked on, a smile on my face.

CHAPTER 4

As soon as I got back to The Pet Library, the smile disappeared. The door, I now realized, I had left unlocked. This might not have mattered; in fact, at first I was relieved that, cage in hand, I wouldn't have to fuss with the keys, and pushing my way in, I said, "Welcome home, Richard." Immediately I sensed a disturbance. I placed Richard's cage on the desk and caught sight of the marmalade cat, tied to a chair with a dog leash, like a prisoner awaiting interrogation. I leaped over and untied him, for which he thanked me not at all, only slunk off, his tail puffed up and bristling. A cat tree lay on the floor, its feather toys torn off; cabinets stood open; on the floor lay canned goods, bags of dog food. "What the hell?" I said.

My first thought was the animal rights people, who for years had been sending Nancy hate mail. In the beginning, she'd thought that she could win them over, naively supposing that she and the animal rights people were on the same side. They would come round ostensibly to inspect the cleanliness of the cages and Nancy would wheedle them to apply for a membership card. But they never so much as checked out a hamster. Instead they organized protests, wrote letters to the newspaper, and once they covered The Pet Library's windows with black spray paint that said, "2-DAY LOAN PERIOD = 2 MUCH TRAUMA." Luckily, *that* wasn't so catchy. Their movement fizzled out when the local leader left to set up a handicraft cooperative in the Kyrgyz Republic.

As I walked around, checking out the damages, I realized I wasn't looking at the work of the animal people. They would have escaped with every animal in tow, and although I hadn't done a head count, already I was conscious of having kicked the rooster away with my boot. Now he was pecking away at a torn bag of dog food, greedily keeping pace with the mutts. The record book was on the floor, a few of its pages bent, but nothing was missing. No, whoever had come in had not wanted to destroy the place. They had vandalized it, almost carelessly. I was wandering around, noting the large amount of water on the floor—did the fish jump out of the tank?—when the door chimed, and Nancy stepped into the room.

She screamed. It was such an awful blood-curdling scream—and not, may I remind you, the first scream I'd heard that day—that I almost wet myself. Her scream was answered by Richard's scream, which was answered by the dogs barking, which was answered by the cats yowling, which was answered by the rooster crowing, which in turn set off a car alarm right outside the door.

"Look this place! What happened? You drink vanilla latte?"

As Nancy darted around the room, taking inventory of the disaster, I felt a hard knot in my stomach, twisting and turning. This was an admirable opportunity to put the Core Values into action—particularly RESOLUTION—but I hardly knew where to begin.

"Where is Willie?" Nancy muttered in a low voice. "Where is poodle?"

"I'm sure he's here somewhere," I said though at that point, I wasn't. It didn't seem likely that anyone would have abducted a poodle, but if the vandals had held the door open for him, he might have run off. He was Nancy's favorite, but not as attached to her as she liked to think.

A whimpering noise came from the back room.

"Willie?" Nancy cried. "Where are you?"

"I know this sounds weird, but he might be tied up," I said, but she had already broken past me before I could finish my sentence.

In fact, he had not been tied up. But neither had he been spared. Whoever had barged into the place had managed to find the electric clippers and shave fluffy white Willie clean as a lamb. It was fascinating to see him shivering there under the table, all white and pink, like a licked candy cane. About three feet away from him lay a soft, enormous, tufty pile of fur.

"William!" said Nancy, stricken.

I wish I could say that was the end of the trouble. In fact, because I had left the fish tank uncovered, the cats had helped themselves to a snack, which explained the water on the floor. It must have taken them quite a bit of work to catch those fish. You might almost say they deserved them—not that Nancy was open to entertaining that point of view.

"You leave fish tank uncovered," she wailed. "Cats loose! Fish massacre!"

"I have a notion," I began. "I feel that my talents are a bit under-used in my present position. I realize that right now you may not even be following every word that I'm saying, but I'll go on. The Pet Library is ailing—admit it! Admit what you and every other person in this town know. This Pet Library is going down. Hard. I reckon we can't compete with companies that sell long-term ownership of dogs and cats and hamsters, et cetera. But what if we offer something different, something less run-of-the-mill than cats and dogs?"

"We do that," Nancy insisted. "We do rooster, we do llama."

"I know. But do we do parrot?" and here I unveiled Richard who, despite his initial echo of Nancy's death cry, had yet to be noticed by her. Then I gestured to the long front windows by which I wanted to build a sandy bank. "I'm thinking seashells, I'm thinking palm trees. Parrots, geckos, maybe a *dif-*

ferent kind of fish tank—one with a wave machine? Nancy Wang, I'm talking about branding the place. Not just any old animal rental, but—are you listening?—*Pets Treasure Island!*"

"Where you get money for parrot?" she asked.

"Well, it's our money. Your money, of course. I took it from the petty cash."

"What petty cash? No petty cash here!"

As I said, I'm no economist, but from what Nancy said next, I gather that the money I'd used had not been ear-marked for the business. Apparently she had been stashing it away for her mother's hip replacement. But she kept it in The Pet Library, so how was I to know? Quite suddenly, Nancy sat—or rather collapsed—on the floor, hugging Willie and crying, her hair sticking in wet wisps to her face. Willie licked her tears.

"I work hard to build Pet Library. People in community say thank you, Nancy. Thank you for bringing animal joy to my life. When I hire you, you say you like animals."

"I told you I was tired of working the gift wrap department at Flounkers. It's not my fault if your English isn't good. Maybe I said I like to *eat* animals."

"You have problem in your head!" she shouted. "Give back money now or I call lawyer! Flighty! You are flighty person!"

"It's all very well to call me names, but I don't *have* your money. I have this parrot. —Oh wait." I fumbled in my pocket and produced two soiled fives and some change. She ungraciously left my hand to dangle in the air. "Nancy," I said, in my kindest voice, hoping to restore the crisis to its proper proportions. "I think you and I have had a misunderstanding about my job description."

She stood up and began to scream in Chinese, causing Willie to pee all over the floor. I shook my head, but before I could explain that it was not *my* job to get a rag, the rooster began to choke on a dog food nugget the size of his trachea. I don't know if you've ever seen a rooster choke, but it's a terrible sight. Even more frightening was the prospect of having to pick up his herky-jerky body and perform the Heimlich maneuver. "Help me, help me!" Nancy ran insensibly through Willie's urine and made her way to the rooster, but I had already grabbed Richard's cage and was hotfooting it out the door.

CHAPTER 5

Back in my studio apartment, I reached for the phone. Could anyone be more lost than I?

I started to call my mother—a reflex reaction when I smell trouble—but before I completed dialing, I realized I had no desire to hear her point of view and saved myself by hanging up. Then I called Lars, who was at work and couldn't take my call, and Rena, who was not, and immediately came over to feed and water Richard. This was fortunate, since I was in no condition to nurture a bird. She insisted she didn't mind.

"You haven't called me in a long time," she said. "So you're still deep into this *Treasure Island* thing, huh?"

"Inch-thick, knee-deep, o'er head and ears, a fork'd one! Thanks for asking. Lately my sister's the only one who asks, but she asks because it's her library copy. She's pissed about the overdue notices."

"Of course. They'll revoke her borrowing privileges!"

"You're as bad as her. They won't. They'll just decide the book is lost. Adrianna wants me to get my own copy, but that's crazy—like telling a superstitious person to buy a new rabbit's foot." I nuzzled the book against my cheek.

"Did you used to have a rabbit's foot when you were a kid?" Rena said, shuddering. "Mine was dyed blue and on a little metal chain. My uncle gave it to me. Whose idea of luck was that? Certainly not the rabbit's."

Rena cut up some banana and gave Richard a water dish, occasionally throwing him flirty little glances.

"I've pet-sat for a Zebra Finch and some lorikeets," she said. "But never a large exotic. He sure seems like a character."

"What's wrong with him?" I said.

"Nothing. I just mean he has a lot of personality."

At that Richard screamed, loosening the fillings in my molars.

"Maybe turn off the maritime music," Rena suggested.

Reluctantly I did, but Richard didn't calm. He screamed and screamed until Lars pressed the buzzer to be let into my apartment. "Wonder why *that* shut him up?" I said as I pressed the intercom. Rena left as Lars entered. In passing they exchanged mildly distressed greetings, Rena clobbering his hip with her enormous Turkish Kilim hand-woven expandable purse.

"I'm not taking sides," Lars said after he had heard, two or three times, my story.

I cuddled up to him on the bed, about three feet from the bird whose cage sat unhygienically on my table.

"Do," I urged. "Do take sides. Otherwise where is the fun?"

"Well, okay, I'm thinking maybe you were out of line a little."

"Oh come on! Nancy thinking I stole her money, *that's* out of line."

"You did take it—"

"But it was petty cash. And I'm her employee. She's putting the worst possible spin on it. She goes about as if she's St. Francis of Assisi! I'm supposed to bring extraordinary diligence to her scrappy endeavor? I said I'd work there, not that I would *live* for the animals. 'Oh, time to feed hamsters!'" I added. "'Oh, time to brush cats!'"

"Please don't do her accent," Lars said, his mouth askew.

"But you know the apple barrel scene, right? Jim Hawkins overhearing Long John Silver plotting a mutiny? After Jim falls asleep in the apple barrel? That's how he discovers half the crew are pirates."

"So?" Lars said, failing to grasp the magnitude.

"So then Jim rushes back to the Captain, Dr. Livesey, and

Squire Trelawney and tells them everything he's just heard. And they're all like, Wow, Jim, with this information you have basically saved our asses, only they put it better. They're complimenting him and the doctor says, 'Jim is a noticing lad.'"

Lars looked at me blankly.

"A noticing lad, a noticing lad," I said, smacking his thigh. "*I'm* a noticing lad, and that's why I do Nancy's voice. I've *noticed* that Nancy talks without any articles."

Lars has a bit of fight in him, so long as the topic isn't too personal. "You told me Nancy's lived in the States twelve years. She owns her own business. She's probably more integrated in the community than *we* are. No way she sounds like a Chinese stereotype."

"But you haven't met Nancy," I grumbled. "She really does talk like that. One day I'll go to China and the native speakers can quote my egregious errors as much as they want—then you'll see."

"Since when are *you* going to China?" Lars said with a touch of sulkiness. That's when it hit me: Lars wasn't politically sensitive, not by a long sea mile. He was afraid I'd leave him.

"Don't worry, I'm not planning any trips. Unless someone does all the arrangements for me, flight and hotel and all that, I don't even *like* to travel."

"Scrraww!" Richard said. Wings flat, head tucked, he appeared to be molesting his feathers.

"You know what Nancy's really upset about? Willie. But it wasn't me who shaved him. Who do you think *did* pick up those clippers?"

"I have no idea. Maybe some kids wandered in and then did it for a prank—"

"Teenagers!" I remembered the boys speeding past me in the mud-splashed car. I had waved to them. Willie's tormentors.

"Do you have another job in mind?" Lars asked.

"What?" I said, caught unawares.

"That's why I'm thinking you should talk to Nancy. Face to face. BOLDNESS. KINDNESS. FORGIVENESS—"

"Lars, you don't even relish the adventure, do you? You're like Tom Redruth, the gamekeeper who gets dragged along, and grumbles the whole time."

"Doesn't ring a bell."

"Heart of gold; not a lot of drive; eats a bullet in Chapter Twenty-Five: The Attack. Besides, there's nothing about *forgiveness* in the Core Values! Jesus. Read the book!"

But the longer we sat on my bed, in my lovely studio apartment, with its cheerful, flimsy sub-Urban Outfitters furnishings, the more I realized I had no savings and would rather slit my wrists than go back to the gift wrap department at Flounkers. At least at The Pet Library I could read. And maybe Nancy could take the parrot back.

"Lars, hand me my stationery box."

At first, I chose a lovely medium-weight note-card with a letter-pressed border of red peonies, a piece of stationery that came from a superb out-of-town paper boutique. Just imagining Nancy's hands (never manicured) unwrapping it on the counter (invariably soiled) prompted me to save the card for a better occasion. Here was a dull card with fern fronds, leftover from a box set. I drew a thick decorative swirl over the "Thank You" and it was perfect.

Dear Nancy, I wrote. Immediately an image sprung up of her sifting through the mail in the back room, the airbrushed centerfold of cats warping off the wall behind her. *Since you've misconstrued my actions, I'm bound by my honor to explain them. Many, many times I looked at The Pet Library's petty cash and thought of how I could use the money for my personal uses, for instance to buy a cashmere sweater—which I'm fairly sure I'm never going to be able to buy—and yet I didn't. I hope I'm right when I say that this kind of restraint counts for something. I took the money to buy a parrot for The Pet Library. Which wasn't right, my boyfriend tells me now, but wasn't the most wrong thing in the world either, as it was an act on behalf of the business and not a misappropriation of funds for a personal sweater. I had no idea the money didn't belong to The Pet Library. As for the fish, I wish I hadn't left the tank uncovered but you can hardly blame the cats for taking a crack at them. When Jim Hawkins counts up the dead after the first skirmish, the crew has been reduced from nineteen to fifteen. And two more wounded, lying about, I think. But he soldiers on. As for Willie his coat was his best feature but, on the bright side, it will grow back, and now it will be easier to really go after his eczema. I hope you accept this apology and let me know at your earliest convenience about my hours for the coming week. I could work this Saturday, but not Sunday because Lars and I have plans and I was going to ask you, before you fired me, if I could have Wednesday off. Any of the other usual hours would be good.*

Your Faithful Hand

Sometimes when a person does something wrong, she finds it easier to continue in a wrong way; for if having done a wrong thing, she proceeds to do a right thing, the wrong thing may appear to others all the more plain. I offer this sententiousness as an attempt to understand Nancy, whose actions the most compassionate person would find difficult to explain. Not only did she fire her best and only part-time employee, she refused to accept Richard for her collection. This woman who for years had given homes to lizards that people had dumped anonymously into the drop-box after maiming them, *refused*, as a matter of principle, to accept my bird. All she wanted was her money back.

I was at my parents' house, explaining some of the indignities to my sister Adrianna, who for financial reasons, had recently moved back home. Adrianna loaded pita chips with hummus and ate them very slowly, leaning one elbow on the speckled Corian breakfast bar.

"Well, he's yours now," she said. "Tell me where you see potential snags."

I counted them off on my fingers.

"The dirty cage. The smell of feather dust. The cost of feed. The cost of shots. Holding the bird for shots. The bird angry with me after shots. Daily upkeep. Daily training. Daily contact." I paused and stared at my pinky. "There's also the question of how I could own a bird and ever go away on the weekends."

"You never go away on the weekends. You come over to Mom and Dad's."

"Well, maybe I've been *planning* to go away on weekends."

"Maybe it would be good for you to have a pet," Adrianna said. "The responsibility, I mean. Besides, if you needed to get away, doesn't your friend Rena do pet-sitting?"

I passed myself the tub of hummus she'd been hoarding.

"Rena gets on my nerves."

Adrianna looked quizzical.

"Very unambitious personally, and very doom-and-gloom about the environment. Mm thinking of cutting her loose," I said with a full mouth.

"She still worried about her nitrogen footprint?"

"Negative energy," I summarized. A huge glob of hummus dropped onto my mother's vinyl coupon organizer, which was lying on the counter. "Let's finish talking about Nancy. Do you understand what I've sacrificed for her, how much study of *Treasure Island* I've missed while I sat and signed out her goldfish? I was trying to help her. Now I wonder where I'd be if I'd applied my ingenuity to myself instead of to her Library."

"There's an idea."

"The real reason Nancy hates the parrot is because she doesn't have the guts to go and get *anything* for the Library."

"But it's the money issue too, right? She'd been saving up for her mother's hip replacement."

In the pantry, packed with chickpeas, Cheez-its, and peanut butter pretzels for my parents' next two hundred guests (they never entertained), I found and broke open a second bag of chips.

"If I have to, I'll keep Richard even if it ruins me, even if I have no money to go to the movies or buy clothes or ever go anywhere on the weekend ever. But I'll tell you what I told Nancy's voicemail last night: only if she takes the parrot will I let bygones be bygones."

"Who's talking about bygones?" my mother said, coming into the kitchen with a basket of laundry.

"Who's picking up fag-ends of conversations?" I said.

She set her basket down on the kitchen table and, as if I had said nothing at all, began to fold my father's boxers.

"I mean, who's pulling on the line? Dipping without a chip? Fishing without the bait? Cruising without a motor?"

"Really, sweetie, I have no idea what you're talking about."

"Exactly," I said. "Because I wasn't talking to you. I was talking to Adrianna."

"Oh," my mother said, with the pleasure of having successfully translated a scrap of a foreign language, "have I interrupted?"

"Well, yes. It was kind of a confidential matter."

"Okey dokey." She took her laundry down the hallway and disappeared into her bedroom.

"What was all *that* about?" Adrianna said. "You pissed at Mom?"

"I'm not pissed. I just don't need her knowing my business. Listen," I said, when I was sure we were in no danger of being overheard. "You don't happen to have a thousand dollars lying around, do you? That I could borrow?"

With a scornful glance, Adrianna plunged a shard of pita into the hummus.

CHAPTER 7

I've decided to live with Lars," I told Rena on the telephone.

"Really? I thought you were . . . feeling alienated and . . . thinking of breaking up with him. How did this happen?"

"What do you mean, happen? We've been together for five months. Actually, nine, if you count that impromptu sleep-over."

"Yes, but . . . Well, how does he feel about it?"

"He's thrilled. He's more domestic than I am. This is what he's always wanted. Also, I can't pay the rent on my studio."

In an intimate booth at Diamond Dave's Taco Co., Lars had looked at me over the rim of his large-bowled margarita. "You mean you want us to get a place together?"

"Do you mind me asking?"

"Frankly, it's a relief to not be the one doing all the emotional work," he said. "I didn't see it coming though. You've been kind of bitchy lately."

"Preoccupied," I amended. *"Mea culpa."*

"Wow," said Rena on the telephone, after I had explained my plan to immediately move in to Lars's recently renovated sublet one-bedroom condo. "Did you even—I mean, did you try asking your family for help?"

"Well, duh, because what's the fourth Core Value, Rena?"

HORN-BLOWING?"

"That's four. I meant three. What's the third Core Value? INDEPENDENCE. Adrianna has no money, only credit card bills.

Aunt Boothie already paid for the parrot, and my parents will only loan me money with interest. I still owe them money for the Lasik."

"Tough love," Rena said. "Still, what would be the APR?"

"The hell if I know," I said. "I'm not an economist."

In the beginning, living with Lars was lovely. It didn't matter if I was kissing him hello, or kissing him goodbye, or reminding him to pay the bill for cable; there was something sweet in all we did, something fresh and fragrant, as if a spring breeze blew through the apartment, which of course it didn't because it was autumn and I kept all the windows closed even when it was warm so I could enjoy the central air conditioning.

Rena threw out her skepticism and gave us a box of personalized address labels. My mother sent us a congratulatory note and a three and half gallon bucket of caramel corn. Adrianna came over for spaghetti and did a decent impression of not being jealous that I had a live-in boyfriend and she had a loveless life in which her richest emotional engagements were with third graders. Did I mention that since her debt debacle, Adrianna had been living with my parents?

I hadn't wanted to take full ownership of Richard, but now that I was living with Lars, it didn't seem exactly like I had. Richard was *our* baby. After we discovered that Lars's gag reflex was weaker than mine, Lars took to cleaning the cage, and I volunteered to do food and water. I found an independent supply shop not far from the apartment, which seemed a remarkable stroke of good fortune, until I discovered it was owned by a drab and lonely lunatic with strong ideas about avian diet. "I won't sell you vitamins," she said, flitting about the shop like Ben Gunn, prying bottles from my hand. "You need to be thinking about *whole foods*. A green vegetable, an orange vegetable, whatever fruits and vegetables are available seasonally! Sprouts? Yes! Loaded with enzymes! Grow organic and just *wait* till you see the shine of his plumage!" Shine this, I thought and took the bus to PETCO, where I bought a bag of Vita-Mix pellets—and on, second, indulgent thought, a bag of sunflower seeds to motivate Richard during lessons. I now spent my jobless hours training him to speak.

"No, honey, don't let him out," I told Lars, "I know more about animal behavior than you. A cage is a bird's home. It safeguards him from the overwhelming complexity of the world. Letting him out for some exercise would be like throwing a person off a cruise ship for a little swim."

"People swim off cruise ships all the time," Lars said and he began to take Richard regularly on his arm. Sometimes Richard made thrumming noises while he clowned around with Lars's glasses. Sometimes Lars tickled his belly, and Richard made a weird sound like two cups of gravel in a blender, which Lars called laughing.

"See?" said Lars. "Happy bird! See?"

The two of them had such a good time I might have been jealous, except I didn't want the bird to sit on me. The sharp beak. The black tongue. The scaly claws. Ugh!

"Don't let him vent on my index cards," I said. "And if he gets anywhere near my new bag, I'll kill you." My calfskin bag boasted two small side pockets and a main compartment exactly big enough for *Treasure Island*. Rolled leather handles; turn-lock enclosure.

"Maybe you resent him because he cost you your job," Lars said as he walked around the room in big figure eights.

"*That* job? Are you kidding?"

I resented Richard for other reasons. He screamed frequently and imitated Lars's morning cough. A white fungus stippled his beak.

"You can take that off with a little soap and water," Lars said.

"I don't want to coddle him, I'm sure birds in the wild have it. But what in the world should I do about the talking?"

Richard had proved to be a fine mimic, but he favored the voices he heard on the television, which I kept on to overcome the tedium of his lessons.

"Steer the boat, girlfriend," I said.

"It's big, it's hot, it's back!"

"Steer the boat, girlfriend."

"Fall blowout carpet sale!"

"Steer the boat, girlfriend. I'm speaking loud enough, aren't I?"

"You always do," Lars said.

"There's *nothing* in *Treasure Island* about how the parrot begins to talk. No tips at all on the learning process."

"It's a story, not a user's manual. But don't give up, you've got time. Parrots can live for a hundred years, you know."

A hundred years? I glimpsed myself grown old. With a liver-spotted hand, I reached out for the birdseed; an empty house, a funeral procession, Richard on a stranger's arm, flapping his wings on my grave. These images cooled my fervor for the project. One afternoon when the bird let loose a familiar torrent of enthusiasm about a hot double beef patty stacked with cheese, I threw down my book and glared. It was the middle of the day. I covered his cage with the cloth.

"There. Now you'll let me read."

"Scrrraw," he said softly and then quickly fell asleep.

A few hours later, as I rifled through Lars's desk in search of photos, letters, and ticket stubs from his previous girl-friends, the quiet apartment began to feel like a tomb in which I had been buried alive. The autumnal light, the sound of Richard grinding his beak. But at six o'clock, the door burst open, and there was my boyfriend with a bag of dinner in hand. How I leapt from the sofa, how I forgot the indeterminate contents of the desk, how we clung to each other like newlyweds! The sofa that had seemed a desolate raft in the sea of his absence now became a schooner in which we glided, watching television, eating fried food, and kissing each other's ears.

CHAPTER 8

I don't have the training," I said to Rena in the coffee house. "I love cake decorating, but to actually get a job, I'd have to go to pastry school and learn fondant and . . . tart doughs and . . . petit fours."

"Well, maybe you'd like that," Rena said.

"Right now I'm liking the freedom of being cut loose from the job, and the lease on my studio, and the old expectations! I can't describe it. When Henry James read *Treasure Island*, he wrote Stevenson a fan letter and said, 'I feel like a boy again!' Exactly how I feel, but I never was a boy. I'm giddy, can you tell?"

"Too much sugar, maybe." Rena looked down at the bill and flushed. "Speaking of which, I think she forgot to charge us for a coffee. No, there it is. Oh, well." Gloomily, she slid a twenty-dollar bill on top of the check. "How's Richard? Did you bring pictures?"

"Was it you who said a pet would be good for me? The responsibility? Maybe it was Adrianna's half-brained idea. He's a drag. Every time he fails, it's like I'm failing. I say, 'Steer the boat, girlfriend' twenty times and he looks at me like I'm part of his seed tray."

"Birds like seeds."

"I've pretty much given up on him for decent conversation. But I don't like the way he follows me around the apartment with his eyes. It's creepy, how he always seems to be looking. He sits on his perch and stares—like this." I goggled my eyes and willed my nose to appear like a sharp hard beak. "I used to read *Treasure Island* out loud, but he inhibits me."

Rena took the sugar dispenser out of my hand.

"Pets have to be chosen with care. It's not like buying a pair of shoes or something. Which reminds me, where'd you get that bag?"

"Anniversary present from Lars."

A flurry of activity as I showed her the contrast stitching and the side pockets that held my index cards on *Treasure Island*.

"Don't think *he* chose it, Rena. He was going to get flowers. I redirected him."

"I'd get a bag like that if it was vegan," Rena sighed.

"Poor Rena," I said to Lars as we sat on the couch and pulled apart our chopsticks. "Yesterday she pretended not to like my bag because it wasn't vegan, when the truth is she can't afford anything like this because she works as a pet-sitter. Have you ever seen her put on that act? The holier-than-thou voluntary vow of poverty to save the animals thing?"

"She's always been anxious about money," Lars observed. He tipped half the carton of egg foo yong onto my plate.

"Next time let's not bother with the plates," I said.

"The boat!" said Richard.

Lars and I turned to each other in amazement. I gripped his shoulder.

"Did you hear that? I'm going to cry!"

"Pay-off time," Lars said, serenely lifting to his mouth a greasy bundle of noodles.

I peered into the cage. "Again! You can do it!" Richard gazed into the distance and after a moment, raised his tail feathers and excreted something slimy.

I slunk back to the couch and picked up my chopsticks.

"Seeing Rena made me realize I don't want to rush back

into a meaningless job just to pay the utility bill. It isn't worth it. I have bad dreams about the wrong kind of job."

"What kind of dreams?"

In one I sat in the secretary pool at Leonard Milkins Middle School, where my father teaches Latin. In another I was making out with my mother when I had been hired to do yard work.

"They're too boring to describe. I go to work with my dad. When I first read the book I dreamed every night I was Jim Hawkins. Clearly I've strayed. I think my unconscious mind is trying to warn me to stay unemployed a while."

"*Boat!*" Lars repeated and I thought, Why, he's as proud as I am.

"To Richard," I toasted, "our baby bird who's finally learning!"

"Here's to ourselves!"

"Here's to ourselves," I repeated, "and hold your luff, plenty of prizes and plenty of duff! And here's to me and my state of creative unrest!"

I expected Lars to say something else, but he only puckered his forehead and drank.

CHAPTER 9

S ometimes I consider BOLDNESS a quality one has or does not have; other times I think of BOLDNESS as a quality one chooses to cultivate or to let wither on the vine. To avoid thinking in that simplest of dichotomies—bold, not bold—I try to imagine a continuum on which persons of varying degrees of BOLDNESS may be arranged. Unfortunately, the longer I lived with Lars, the more clearly it came to my attention, like a hangnail one feels smarting and tries not to bite, that Lars didn't exemplify even the far far other end of BOLDNESS; in fact on the continuum of BOLDNESS, Lars was off the line.

Boldness Perceived as a Continuum

Boldness—Impudence—Self-Reliance—Timidity—Cowardice • *Lars!!!*

Every day he trailed off to the same low-paying techie support job he'd done since graduating college.

"Isn't it time you made your move?"

"What move?" he said.

"Onward! Upward!"

But he never responded well to such suggestions, insisting that he liked his job, liked talking to people and figuring out problems. One morning when I pressed him to seek out opportunities for advancement, cheer-leading him into a state of energy and self-confidence, exhausting myself at the crumby breakfast table in the hope that he would walk out the door with fresh resolve and make us both proud, he revealed (nonchalantly) that he'd been offered a chance to do something at a software company six months before and passed it up.

And why?

He liked that his job left him "free" on the weekends!

Our weekends, of course, I enjoyed prodigiously; Lars did all the things that I arranged—brunches, shopping, movies. On weekdays, I kept myself in a whirl, partly to avoid missing Lars and partly to insure I didn't stumble back to The Pet Library and beg for my job back. I avoided my parents, knowing they would fail to understand my devotion to *Treasure Island* and worry instead about my outward appearance of inertia. Sometimes my mother would telephone and say, "What are you doing?" "What are *you* doing?" I'd answer, but she never registered the sharpness of my reply. Instead she gave me the record of her accomplishments since rising at six in the morning and outlined, with cheerful precision, her tasks for the rest of the day. "You know me, I like to keep my ducks in a row." I knew what she thought *my* ducks looked like—scattered round the pond, wings drooping, heads listing; one call to Animal Patrol would confirm they had West Nile virus. "But what were you doing just now when I called?" I am sure she wanted to catch me out in something frivolous—waxing the hair off my kneecaps, let's say—but I always told her I was studying my book. "And what are you planning to do?" she persisted one day. "Now that you've left The Pet Library?" "Who knows," I said bitterly, "But I will never be a Latin teacher!" She denied that she had ever harbored the expectation; oh yes, she pretended to be amazed. "We never expected you to follow in Daddy's footsteps. Whatever you want to do, that's what you should do, darling. We've never expected anything from you or Adrianna." True, in that they certainly never *helped* me to do anything.

When this kind of conversation put me into a funk, I bounced around town, picking up niceties for our home and little masculine luxuries for Lars (shaving creams, foot massager, new lizard watch band), and I had time to attend to my own appearance, too, so between the haircuts and eyebrow waxes and cheap Asian manicures, I'd never looked better in my life.

"But listen," Lars said one morning, "I've been looking over the credit card bill and I think we need to cool it a while. Maybe it's just too many take-outs, and we could cook more. The thing is, this is the first time I haven't been able to pay off my monthly balance."

"Lars, you don't have to pay off the monthly balance!" I kissed his unsmiling mouth. "That's why they call it credit."

Lars pulled back from my kiss; we were in the living room and he didn't like to start anything near Richard. Not that the bedroom was much better; one blood-curdling scream and Lars's erection would take French leave. As I kissed him again, he responded with demeaning ambivalence. One hand groped me; the other made placating gestures to Richard, who'd begun to scream.

"Lars," I hissed. "Stop talking to him."

"Wasn't talking. Was just, you know, indicating, that everything's okay. His back feathers ruffled."

We glared at each other.

"He gets upset," Lars added.

"Scrrraaaawww!" Richard said.

"Jesus," I said. "I don't feel like kissing *now*."

"That's okay. That's totally cool. No problem."

"No problem?"

"No problem!" he repeated cheerfully.

Of course, there *were* problems, but the problems were seated beyond the reach of argument—way out in some rural zone where there isn't even Internet access. I tried to handle

Lars with care, as if civility could make up for the deficits, but time stripped our verdant orchard of its leaves. Picture us on a stage with a skeletal Beckett-like tree. Clearly the underlying issue was that Lars didn't want me to change.

"I like your hair the way it is," he said when he heard me on the phone, making a color appointment.

Lars didn't want me to grow.

"You look great," he said, often without even looking.

One Saturday when actively weeding through my wardrobe to make the final decision on what to discard, I allowed Lars to come upon me in a butternut squash sweater and a pair of red corduroy pants.

"That's a nice sweater," he said. "Is it new?"

"This is a filthy old sweater I've had since eleventh grade. It's made of rayon."

"Oh."

"Do you like it?"

"Yes."

"Do you like it with these pants?"

"Yes."

"Even though the colors clash?"

"Yes."

"Even though the pants are baggy in the butt?"

"It looks good on you," he said.

Which was supposed to be a compliment, but in its refusal to engage reality was more accurately the verbal equivalent of a chuck on the chin. I knew very well what Lars meant when he praised me, and held me, and indicated through a caress that he liked me *just the way I was*; I knew, better than he knew himself, that he wanted to ensure he never be confronted with what, in his own personality, might need pruning or pushing or prodding, that behind every show of support he gave, for me here, for me now, there lurked a terrified refusal to acknowledge his own potential to grow. With each endearment, with each endorsement, he tried to make me slack. Did I buckle? Dear Reader, no. I saw his white-knuckled terror, his toes clenching the edge of a perceived abyss, even when he leaned over the garbage bag of clothes and planted a kiss on my head!!

CHAPTER 10

A nd now for the secret autobiography, the chamber within the chamber, the revolving bookcase that spins into a red velvet study, the roomy compartment behind the false back of a tiny drawer.

It is possible to think of my life, up to the age of twenty-five, as a series of therapists I successfully dodged.

"A series of therapists!" you will exclaim.

When I began this story, I had thought to keep my counseling history a secret, but the more I write, the more I think of my reader as a friend with whom I can lounge in even the sour-smelling rooms of the family manse. So here they are, all failures!

1) Dee Bissell-Ivy: Wore her hair in a bun, kept dolls on her shelves
2) Peter Johnson: hush-voiced, still in training, borrowed folding chairs
3) Deborah Grady: red-faced, aggressive, hobby-oriented
4) Jennifer Shaftal: Long-legged, deep tan; began each session by asking if I treated my body like a temple, then proceeded to confuse me with another patient whose parents had repeatedly locked her up in an RV
5) Brenda Pickens: fluffy-haired, fluffy-sweatered, said all "her girls" were hindered by terrible self-esteem

A haze descends when I try to recall the others' names. I ran through every therapist available in that long college hall of Harris Center known as PERSONAL COUNSELING. You could have six free sessions with anyone, and then if dissatisfied, pick a new person and start counting towards your six free sessions again. I never paid for a seventh session with any of them.

In my twenty-fifth year, I was happier and stronger than ever, done with therapists—*finis!*—and yet occasionally I craved a pill to calm my nerves. Where was I in this story proper? Oh yes, I was living with Lars. Notice how closely that sounds like living with lies. It sounds exactly like it, if you imagine yourself saying it with some kind of Eastern European accent. And I *was* living with lies when I was living with Lars. For reasons already apparent, I found myself happy to be rid of The Pet Library but unsteadied by the new arrangements. Now that Lars had gotten tight-fisted, we went to fewer restaurants, and rather than go shopping on weekdays, I spent long lugubrious hours at home, the vapors of which could be dispelled only by picking quarrels. Sometimes I fought lucidly, poignantly, my complaints so beautifully orchestrated I wished I could fight Lars for a living. Other times the quarrels left me confused rather than ennobled; that time I stood in my bathrobe with zit cream on my face and hollered, "Lars, I didn't marry you so you could work at the computer support desk your whole life," especially comes to mind.

"What?" Lars said. "What? You didn't marry me at all!"

"I know. But what exactly are we doing here every night, cuddling up on the couch with a box of General Tsao's chicken?"

The truth was I felt as though I had married him. I'd forgotten that I had strong-armed my way into his apartment because I needed a place to live while I pursued the insights of *Treasure Island.*

Did he want me to leave?

"Maybe I do. Maybe I want a divorce," he said ironically.

Not long after that conversation, I dropped by my mother's internist to get a prescription for a calming pill. My mother's doctor, a half-retired guy named Dr. Rattner, refused to see me, but the secretary said she could squeeze me in to see his partner, Dr. Klug. I don't know why, but when the rap came on the examination door, I was expecting Dr. Rattner's wizened twin to walk in. Instead a chisel-cheeked, healthy, blonde woman, ten years my senior, stood at the foot of the table, ordering me to swing up my feet. I swung them (gladly).

Chest, lung, nose, ears, throat. She smelled like rubbing alcohol and verbena. Why was she examining me, I wondered.

"What do you want pills for?"

"Anxious. Can't sleep."

"You look well-rested. Something bothering you?"

"Yes, no."

"Lie back, please. I don't like to throw a person pills until they've tried other options. Lie back, please. Have you talked to anyone about why you're anxious?"

This was just the opening I needed—and although it was a pretty narrow gap, I shot through it like a winged termite. Rooting *Treasure Island* out of my bag, I told Dr. Klug my theory that there are basically two kinds of people in this world—"those who sail the ship—and that includes sailors, pirates, and cabin boys—and those who cling fearfully to the ship's base. That would be the barnacles."

"Marine biology. It's been a while . . . "

"Never mind, it's a metaphor." Surprisingly, steering the conversation away from that metaphor led me to explain a night in college when I found myself in the student union, pretending to know what *veni, vidi, vici* meant, and to a longer explanation of why I felt hampered by my family, unable to imagine myself casting any shadow in this world at all, except by their lanterns. "The thing is if I am going to become a Latin teacher I would have to go back to school, in my late twenties, and get a lot of Latin down." I explained one of my favorite parts of *Treasure Island*, the bit where Jim Hawkins kisses his mother goodbye, and how, stumbling upon that sequin, I'd realized that, if you talk to your mother every other day, chances are you're not going to *have* an adventure; you have to get away from your cove and open yourself up to strangers. Then, without wanting to go into the whole rationale about why I went to college only fifteen miles from home and after graduation settled in the same town as my parents, I managed to impart a certain amount of personal history and bring the conversation back to the barnacle, by saying my primary goal right now was to peel myself off my ship's bottom—but here I broke off. Lars's mother, when she used to bathe the children, called his sister's butt her "bottom" and her vulva her "front bottom," a euphemism that appalled me, as did the fact that, even though in *my* family we had struck strictly to clinical terms, my recent intimacy with Lars, who calls his penis his "Johnson," had allowed his family language to insinuate itself into my consciousness. This is the best way I can explain why the blood rushed to my face as I heard myself saying "*my ship's bottom*," and I felt obscurely, but acutely, as though I had just asked Dr. Klug to think about what Lars would call my "nether lips." (He thinks he's worldly because his vocabulary evolved away from "front bottom." But the apple doesn't fall far from the tree.)

Dr. Klug nodded. "You do seem anxious. You shredded your gown."

"Well, it takes an awful lot of energy to give birth to oneself. It's not as though you do one bold thing and then you *are* bold. The thing about adventure is that you have to keep on doing it, day in and day out. I don't know, can it ever be definitively accomplished? I hardly rest, I hardly can!"

Dr. Klug nodded slowly. I had a very good feeling about her; I liked her so much I thought I might come talk to her now and then, the way Jim Hawkins strikes up a friendship with Dr. Livesey, whose bright black eyes and pleasant manners contrast with "the coltish folk" around him, though in my case, I might better say "doltish." Dr. Klug replied that she was a doctor of internal medicine, that the best doctor for me to talk to would be a therapist, that there were many qualified therapists in town, that it was kind of me to be concerned but it wasn't a question of her not having the courage to be a therapist, she had always wanted to be an internist, and that I should ask her a different question because she had already told me she wasn't a therapist; and when I said I had no other questions, she left, abruptly, the room.

In the waiting room, the receptionist asked me, with a frankness I found off-putting, how I wanted to pay.

"You have my mom's address. Did the doctor leave me a prescription?"

She hadn't. Had there been a mistake? No. Then there would be no pills? No, the receptionist said, but Dr. Klug would be happy to refer me to a psychiatrist. I didn't want a psychiatrist, I explained, I wanted a sample.

"You guys are supposed to be giving it away like candy. Come on, I bet you have a closet full of starter packages. Please don't pretend Dr. Klug is the only doctor in America not in the drug companies' pocket!"

"I beg your *pardon*?" the receptionist said, as if my pardon were an ugly damp thing and the only possession I had.

"You heard what I said" (after I walked out).

For a few moments I stood quaking in the elevator, unsure of which button to press. Eventually a stoop-shouldered old lady stepped in and pressed "L." Why were the simplest encounters complicated for me? I had trusted Dr. Klug with my personal history and she had repulsed me like she would have any other patient. It was enough to make a person feel . . . generic. I worked myself up to a high level of disgust as the elevator worked its way down to the low level of the lobby. When the doors chortled open, the sun-struck, airy atrium broke the elevator's gloomy ambience. My elderly companion hustled out before I could even make a show of letting her go first.

"I got a doctor's bill for you from Rattner's office," my mother said. "I hadn't known you were sick."

"No, I wasn't," I said carelessly. "I just wanted to go for a check-up."

"Well, next time, let's talk about it first. You're not on Daddy's insurance. When you get a job—"

"I'm fine now. Actually, I'm exploring alternative kinds of medicine."

For my mother the phrase "alternative medicine" registered only as some kind of youth-culture slang. "Really? Well, good for you. It's so important to have a hobby."

Lars hardly understood it either. "Why are you going for a healing?" he said. At this point we no longer spoke openly about our schedules, but I had left a portrait of my new friend, crisply drawn, on a doodle pad, under which I'd written, absent-mindedly, in a fine cursive sprawl, *Beverly Flowers Personal Healer Beverly Flowers Personal Healer Beverly Flowers Personal Healer*. Also I had used the page to blot up some spilled coffee, and now, a few days later, Lars was finally getting around to cleaning up the mess.

"She's a remarkable woman, if you have to know."

I had known this the first time I set foot in her office. Bev Flowers looked to be in her early fifties, and her rooms were elegantly furnished in a grey and green color scheme, as if to suggest the mossy underside of a stone. She greeted me honorably, as if I were a soldier just back from the war, and as we faced each other on matching Indonesian chairs, she was so attentive I thought I might weep. So this is what it was like to be around a spiritual person. I fished *Treasure Island* out of my bag and laid it on my knees.

"Every hour alone with this book helps fortify me. I'm cast away, like Ben Gunn on the island, only I'm in our apartment, and instead of powder and shot . . . "

"Maybe"—Bev pressed her hand against the book and cocked her head—"Maybe this book has a higher vibration."

"Exactly! Yes!" My relief was so intense, I wanted to stand up and punch a hole through the rice paper screen that divided the room. Instead I signed up for Beverly Flowers's package deal, six one-hour healing sessions and three long-distance attunements.

"But are you sick?"

"You don't have to be 'sick' to undergo a healing," I told Lars. "You just have to be open to a life-source of positive energy."

"It's big, it's hot, it's back!" Richard shrieked.

Lars threaded his way through the apartment, collecting dirty plates and crumpled-up napkins.

"Shut up!" I hurled an empty tuna can at Richard. It missed widely, but the way he carried on, you would have thought I punctured his crop, and Lars, who never threw anything at Richard, looked ready to reprimand me. Instead he turned around, picked up the can and tossed it into the garbage.

"Stupid bird!" I said as the parrot pecked his dirty feathers.

Lars gave a sort of sigh.

"Idiotic non-stop-talking feather duster!"

"Did you notice he's not talking? You scared him."

I found this information hard to digest—and weirdly exciting, too. I had spent so much time being afraid of Richard. All these weeks he had seemed stolid and indifferent—capable of antagonizing me, but not capable of being hurt. Was it possible the tables were beginning to turn and he, in fact, was cowed by me? If a bird can be cowed, I mean.

"Who knows?" Lars said. "Why don't you run it by the healer?"

I might have—despite his sarcasm, I truly might have—but the next time I saw Bev Flowers she didn't want to chat.

"Lie down on the table," Bev said. "I want to check your energy fields right away."

Fieldwork promised great things. I'd been told how another client smelled burnt tapioca all over the room when Bev checked her energy fields; another woman gasped as an umber aura shuddered down her torso; a third client swore she heard frogs. I hadn't sensed anything yet, but today might be different, I thought as I closed my eyes; given Bev's urgency, today might be the day I . . .

I fell asleep.

When I woke up, the rice paper screen had been moved and Bev was arranging a tea tray. She gestured for me to join her and folded her hands in her lap.

"How am I?" I asked after a moment.

"Your anchor has been dropped," Bev said. "The boat is going nowhere. I realigned your energy fields but I'm concerned you're not progressing." She poured the tea, which was deep yellow and smelled of grass. "The book," she began.

Bev had a strong streak of renunciation. The last session she had pressed me to give up coffee, sugar, and wheat. I pushed back my chair.

"I won't give it up."

"I wouldn't ask you to. I just want you to imagine that you're obsessed, not with a book—but with a man. You wouldn't tense to enjoy him; you would soften." Bev tipped her head back and offered her neck to an imaginary lover. It was disturbing since I'd never seen her in any remotely sexual posture. Usually we talked about the spirit in nautical terms.

"A man? Oh, no. No, no . . . "

"I once read *Treasure Island*. This didn't seem relevant to your healing when you first came in. In fact, it was years ago, I was reading it to my son. Well, there are many things about me . . . " She waved her hand, as if to disperse information she had momentarily thought of sharing. "Back then he was a boy, and like you, very interested in pirates."

I suppressed a flicker of irritation.

"Did he like it?" I asked.

"Yes."

"And you liked it?"

"Yes."

I pulled my chair closer in.

"But I don't remember the Johns Hopkins you focus on in your meditations."

"Jim Hawkins."

"I don't remember a bold, resolute, independent boy."

"HORN-BLOWING. I wrote this down for you. The fourth one is HORN-BLOWING."

"Who is the charismatic sea cook, the great betrayer, the guy with a wooden leg?"

I spoke dully: "Long John Silver?"

"Yes! Now there's the center of your novel. Charismatic personality, repellent morally speaking, and it's amazing how he gets around on that one leg. Remember? Jim knows he should be wary of Silver, but he's drawn to him for good reasons."

"Lars is all right," I said after a pause. "He's got no prosthetics and there's nothing *deadly* attractive about him. I always wish he'd pluck those nose hairs."

Bev exhaled and looked like a glass that somebody had picked up and drained. I wanted to ask her more, but knew my cue to go. We hugged; she was a spiritual mother, only thinner and better smelling than I ever expected a spiritual mother to be. But as I walked home, her remarks about *Treasure Island* hung like a dark cloud over my mind. I have never cared at all for Long John Silver; to me he is like the annoying uncle at a family party to whom one talks for a few minutes and then, if one has any sense, claps one's eye on Aunt Boothie in the middle distance and squeezes past. Could Bev really think *Treasure Island* was about *him*? It was because I liked Bev so much that I wanted us to agree. Also because I was paying her a hunk of money for the healings.

I lay on the sofa and gloomed.

What if I was paying the wrong person to heal me? Surely it was wrong to let a person enamored with Long John Silver realign my energy fields when Jim Hawkins was the one who carried the mother-lode. The day wore on and in my mind's dispassionate eye I saw myself on the massage table, wrestling Beverly Flowers for control of my soul. For weeks I had gloated about the power of her touch, the dignity of her bearing, the feminine fit of her suede shirt—and now I thought, I am a fool, a fool, to sail unwittingly into such a dangerous cove. If Beverly Flowers bent my spirit out of whack, how would I even know it? I can't check my energy fields any more than I can check the fuse box in Lars's apartment.

"Don't worry," Lars said when the lights went out. "Though that's the third time this month."

"Did you pay the bill?"

"Of course I paid the bill. It's just the fuse."

Darkness fell like a shroud on the apartment. If Beverly Flowers and my visions were incompatible, what would I do? "He was a boy, and like you, very interested in pirates." I had never said I was interested in pirates! Pirates were beside the point! Mere accessories!

The lights snapped on again.

"All right, I'm going to bed," said Lars.

"You just got the lights back on."

"I have to work tomorrow."

That night I tossed and turned so much that Lars sat up and

asked what was the matter with me, but before I could refine the point he said I had to talk to someone who had read the thing. That's what he called the book: "the thing," as if it were not a masterpiece but a B-grade monster crawling out of a swamp. Then he took the best wool blanket and slept on the couch.

CHAPTER 11

L isten," Rena said in the coffee shop. "There's something I wanted to tell you."

As she tore her napkin into long thin strips, I began to worry she would make some complaint. Of course, I too had felt dissatisfactions about our friendship, ones I could trace back to the dorm when she used to borrow my hairdryer without asking, but at the moment I had no desire—none at all— to analyze our relationship. The very prospect filled me with dread. What if she dragged my character into it? A crust of grilled cheese stuck in my throat.

"I'd better just blurt it out," Rena said. "Nancy called and asked if I would work at The Pet Library, and I said yes. I've been working there for a few weeks."

I put down my sandwich and laughed. "I thought you were going to tell me something horrible! I mean, for me."

"I'm still freelancing, of course, but the Library gives me a steady paycheck."

"Not much of a paycheck. But good for you."

"You don't mind?"

I swept her little strips of napkin into a tidy pile. "Why would I?"

"I didn't know if you were still hoping to patch things up over there, or—"

"I'm through with that job. I wouldn't work there if Nancy paid me. You know what I mean."

"Well, that's what I thought." Rena grew quiet and began

to pick at the callus on her thumb. "Do you remember when your *Treasure Island* thing started, and you kept calling in sick so you could shop for a blouse with a lace jabot?"

"A few times I blew it off, but I hardly think—"

"That's when I first subbed for you. It's not like I *tried* to move in on the job. And I want you to know, when Nancy called and asked for help, I said, 'I wouldn't dream of it, what if she's thinking of coming back?' I only changed my mind when Nancy goes, 'Never in a million years—'"

How dare they? Like girls gossiping behind their hands.

"Rena, it's a dead bush."

"What?"

"A dead horse. Quit beating around the bush. I said I don't mind it."

"All right." She flinched. "Beating a dead horse. What a cruel expression!" After a pause she said, "How's Lars?"

"He's fine."

As we drank our coffee I studied the lithograph above the table as if I had never really seen it before, which in a way I hadn't. It was a boat and a sunset, but the wrong kind of boat—two lovers drifting in a canoe.

Rena reached into her enormous filthy Turkish Kilim hand-woven expandable purse.

"Well, here," she said. "I got the pills you wanted."

A photograph of schnauzers was stuck to the prescription bottle. "Eddie and Neddie and Nod!" Rena's eyes rested on the dogs for a moment with deep affection; then her face went blank and she threw the dogs back into that dark hairy pit of a purse. She slid the bottle across the table.

"You're welcome to these. It's interesting how animals can relax a person. I haven't touched Xanax since I began at the Library. I'll be rearranging the gravel in the fish tank, or combing out the dogs, and I get this extraordinary sense of calm. The feeling can stay with me all day long." Rena gripped

the table stiff-armed as a zombie. "Oh my god! I just remembered! I promised to check on Mrs. Minnelli's box turtle."

I slid the check across the table.

CHAPTER 12

The letter arrived, looking innocuous enough, in a small floral envelope. Lars had picked up the mail as we came in, and began to read the letter in the doorway. He froze in the hall like a flamingo. I had to maneuver around him just to put away my coat.

"I've . . . "

Long pause; he continued to read.

"I've . . . "

"*What*?" I said.

"I've just gotten the strangest letter from my mother. It's bizarre, but I can't figure out . . . what on earth could have . . . why is she so upset?"

"Let me see it."

The letter was written in a crazy hand, cursive loping across the page like antelope across the plain; and from what unseen predator?

"I'm baffled," Lars said. "She's demanding an apology, and yet I don't know what for . . . Who do you think—I can't believe—oh no. Do you think my sister—?"

"Look here, Lars," I said, guiding his distressed person gently to the sofa. "Your mother called the other day when you weren't home, and I took the occasion to have a bit of a talk. I've never felt drawn to your mother, but some intimacy was long overdue. We had a bout of it."

When Lars sunk back against the cushions, I explained what I'd long observed as his extremely fucked-up relationship with his mother, citing among other weirdnesses his habit of calling her every single Saturday at one in the afternoon, and speaking to her for precisely an hour, always about the most superficial things, unless for some reason he was unable to get her on the phone, in which case he insisted on calling her at the same time on Sunday and plodding through his dreary conversational routine then. This mode of communication, which he stubbornly preferred to anything more natural and spontaneous, not only disrupted the easy artless flow of my weekend life, but perpetuated the false relations he'd always had with his mother, a weak-headed but controlling woman whom he'd never risked telling anything that he truly thought, preferring instead to reflect back her own shallow opinions so as to keep himself in her good graces.

This discourse about himself and his mother Lars tried to divert by rising up hastily and insisting that I'd had no right to speak to his mother about private things.

"Well, Lars, the only things I told your mother were things that directly concerned her; opinions of her that you, her son, have been withholding; and though you're upset now—I see your neck is getting that patch of red it always does when you try to suppress a true emotion—once you calm down, you'll thank me for bringing some emotional honesty into your life."

But Lars, who has never been a genius about feelings, accused me of calling up his mother to make trouble. This was a terrible distortion, since his mother had in fact called me.

"'Well,' she says, 'do you think Lars would like a sweater for Christmas?' 'What kind of sweater?' A holiday sweater with fifteen different colors in a crisscrossing acrylic design— but that's not the point. So I say, 'Look, I'm neutral as Sweden on the subject of this sweater, but I do happen to know that Lars has a drawer full of acrylic sweaters you've given him that he never wears; and it's not lost on him that you always give his sister more expensive gifts such as Cheese of the Month Club and electronics.' 'Electronics?' she says. 'That iPod Shuffle,' I remind her. 'And also, some year before that, a clock radio.'"

Lars's frantic mind could not absorb the details as I repeated them.

"Listen to me. You don't know my mother. My mother can't bear to hear that stuff! My mother doesn't go in for honesty! What were you thinking?"

"Lars, you underestimate your mother. She's not a little old lady with a bone china heart. Your family could stand to tell her the truth about all kinds of things."

Lars stared fixedly at a pile of index cards I'd left on the table, but it was clear he wasn't reading them. "At least, by lying a little, we've always managed to get along."

"Lars, I know that letter of your mother's is a good thing. The first honest exchange in your family ever and the start of authentic relations. I saw she called you a 'spoiled brat'—and that seems harsh, but can't you feel the air getting clearer?"

"She called *you* a spoiled brat," Lars said, fingering the letter.

"Really?" I insisted on checking it.

CHAPTER 13

I put your stuff in the basement," Lars said. "I didn't know if you'd be taking it to your parents' right away."

Yes, Reader, Lars had put all of my things into boxes and moved them into that infernal part of his apartment building known as "the cage," a floor to ceiling metal box on the basement level, near to the laundry room, lit by a solitary bulb streaked with dead bugs. Lars didn't store any of his own things there; the overhead pipes dripped incessantly. I stood in a parallelogram of light on the hardwood floor, looking him in the face, pluckily enough to all outward appearance, but inside, miserable.

"Well," I said, "did you put your heart into storage too?"

He didn't answer this directly.

"I've got a key, but it would be better if you called the landlord."

"Is this it, Lars? Aren't you going to tell me what went wrong? Where's the big scene? Where's the show-down?"

"I don't want a showdown. I have no interest in fighting."

What kind of sad sack has no interest in fighting, I asked him. For an instant I sat below deck with the squire and the doctor, a bottle of Spanish wine and some raisins before us, Captain Smollett issuing forth commands. *It would be pleasanter to come to blows. Now, sir, it's got to come to blows. What I propose is to take time by the forelock and come to blows some fine day when they least expect it.* Lars wouldn't fight because he was afraid a fight would make him confront the truth about himself. And so, out of love, I refused to move out.

"Then what did he say?" said Rena when we met at the coffee shop.

"'Today would be good,' he said, but I've got several appointments I need to keep and no desire to disrupt my schedule because his royal Larsness asked me to. He can take the sofa, if my presence really bothers him."

"Wow," breathed Rena.

"I'm pleased with myself for refusing to cave in to his request. You should come on over after this."

"Oh no," Rena said. "I couldn't—"

"Why?"

"Not if it's his place. You know. I think it would be awkward."

"Rena, it's *our* place! Don't be ridiculous."

I was dying for Rena to see how I had begun to enjoy Lars's apartment. My stuff was in banana boxes, but I made use of every thing of his in sight. I wore his favorite bathrobe uncinched, the tie dragging across the dusty floor. I slathered myself with his sensitive skin moisturizer, heated his organic marinara in the microwave and splattered the sauce, used his electric razor and didn't obsessively clean out my hairs.

"Look, are you coming or not?"

"I can't," Rena said. "Between The Pet Library and the pet-sitting, my schedule is crazy."

"I'm sorry to see you so distracted." I pushed the check across the table.

When I got back to the apartment, the phone was ringing. Naturally I pounced on it, thinking it might be Lars.

"Is Lars there?" a woman trilled.

I knew her voice: Chelsea, whose luckless experiences with boyfriends Lars had often, with too much sympathy, detailed.

"You have the wrong number," I said.

"Do I? Is this seven five three—"

"Did you say Lars? Or Louse? Or Lies?"

Then I unplugged the phone—and kept it unplugged, except for when I wanted to use it.

I'm not going to relate every detail of the siege. It was tiring, even with the advantages of the healing sessions, which increased my stamina, and made me think I could hold out forever, until the day when Bev Flowers stopped me in the outer room, by the serenity fountain, and asked me to pay off my balance. "Well, here's the awkward thing," I told Bev. "It's Lars who's been loaning me the money for healings, but now he went and changed his ATM number." "I'm sorry to hear that," Bev said, and that was my last alignment. In the end, Lars chose a cowardly route and called my mother, who could be trusted in a pinch with almost anything. She surmised that the affair between Lars and me was over and recommended that my lingering in the apartment be stopped. In her careful, experienced way, she took care of the peskiest details, even renting a van and helping me to pack.

"Lars, don't make this awkward," I said when it was almost time for me to depart. "My mom's outside. Richard is a good bird and I want you to keep him as a souvenir of what you and I had together."

We were standing in his living room, one of us with a calf-skin bag jauntily slung over her shoulder, the other looking rumpled and depressed in relaxed fit khakis. I wanted him to take the bird, but in no way feel he was doing me a favor.

"Well, if you won't take him as a gift, then take him to square the count. I'm sure I owe you something for these months, and he's the only thing I've got that's worth anything." I shifted the bag on my shoulder.

Lars looked at the floor and shook his head.

"It's funny, Lars, I just got through telling Rena how different you are. I said, Richard's like our child, Lars feeds him and holds him and plays with him, he would never just sail off like he never knew him. 'I don't know,' said Rena. 'You'd be surprised.' 'Come on, Rena,' I said. 'Think about it! Without Lars, whose glasses would Richard peck? I don't wear glasses since the Lasik!' And Rena said—"

From the street came the husky belch of a garbage truck.

I changed tack. "Look, I'll give you fifty bucks if you'll take the bird now, fifty bucks when I get settled, and five bucks a week for upkeep. You're a fool if you don't see you can turn a profit."

"What in god's name are you talking about? I don't want to make a profit!" Lars sank into a chair, whipped off his glasses and buried his face in his hands.

I had seen him do this before—once when his great uncle, three times removed, had had a stroke; and another time when he was peeved at me for not understanding why he'd been so upset that his great uncle, three times removed, had had a stroke (I'd accused him of dramatizing). Then he'd covered his face with his hands for a full minute; now he curled into the posture and remained there, incommunicado, for almost five.

The front door cracked open.

"Halloo?" my mother said. "Oh! Is this a bad time?"

Lars did not remove his face from his hands.

"I came to get the keys to the basement. My goodness, is he all right? Don't let's drive off and leave him like that. Maybe I should call his mother."

"My mother!" Lars said, as if she had thrown a bucket of ice water to break his enchantment. His hands found his glasses, his glasses found his nose; he jumped up and passionately smacked the wall. "Why would anyone call my mother? My mother isn't even speaking to me!"—and then, as if suddenly remembering his manners, he broke off, excused himself, and went into the bedroom. He closed the door, but very quietly.

"Damn! Do you know how close I was to wrapping things up here? I asked you to wait in the van."

"I came to see if there's anything you want me to carry out of the apartment," my mother replied. "To put in that van."

Hurriedly I gave her my fondue pot, my hairdryer, Lars's Foot Fixer, which he never used, the keys to the basement and my calfskin bag, which contained *Treasure Island*. "Don't swing it around like mad," I said.

"I won't."

Lars came out from the bedroom.

"Excuse my recent outburst. I can talk again about the bird."

"That's quite all right," my mother said, as if the tiff had been between him and her. "Do you mind if I have a peek at Richard? I've never actually seen him."

"I thought you were going," I reminded her.

Lars pulled the cloth off the cage.

"It's big, it's hot, it's back!" Richard shrieked.

"Oh my," my mother said. "Look at you!"

She laid down the things I had carefully balanced in her arms.

"He's a beautiful bird," Lars said thoughtfully.

"He's the most beautiful bird I've ever seen!" my mother said. "Aren't you? Yes, yes. I'm a beautiful bird. I'm a beautiful bird. Yes, I am. I have very large wings."

"I thought you were going."

"In a minute," she said, standing at the cage and inhaling Richard's musk as if he were a rose garden.

"Why don't you take Richard out?" Lars said to me—a covertly taunting remark, since Lars was the one who opened the cage. "You need to see you can do it. He's not going to stay in there all day."

My mother said, "Oh go on, sweetheart!"

Richard hulked on his perch, a twitchy brilliant mass of feathers. It took me half a lifetime to lift the latch and swing open the door. Even before he lunged I could tell he was going to sink his lunatic beak into my finger. When he did, I screamed and flung him to the floor. "Cheeseburger!" Richard said, flaring his wings. Then he bouldered up my leg and latched onto my hip.

"For godsakes!"

"Hush," Lars said and removed the bird as if he were quietly pulling a bur from my coat. A demon bur.

"Are you bleeding?" my mother said.

"It's just a nip," Lars answered.

"I'll show *you* a nip, asswipe!"

"I'm going to wait outside." My mother gathered the appliances back into her arms, threw the calfskin bag over her shoulder, and opened the door, which had been left ajar, with her foot. She walked away, keys jangling.

"Asswipe," Lars repeated. "My god, weren't we, like, in love once? I'm still trying to get my mind around how it all went wrong. Did you ever love me? Maybe you just used me."

More blathering on in this vein: the downside of choosing a sensitive boyfriend. Good looking, solvent, *tried* to be sensitive to my needs, but when we broke up, whoa Nelly! It was all about *him*. Feelings, feelings, feelings; out of nowhere a torrent of emotion as if someone had just turned on the Oprah hose, and *then* he sidles over to give me a hug.

I shrank from him. "Look here, are you keeping the bird or not?"

He was not.

Later I learned that he had privately nicknamed me "Hamburger Helpless," owing to my habit of not helping out more around the apartment. But at the time he said nothing about that. We said goodbye, Lars solemn and unbending, me incensed, and then I struggled out the door with Richard's cumbersome cage in my hand. The bird, shocked by the cold winter air, squawked a little as I hit the street. "Shut up," I said. It consoled me to think I was draining two-thirds of the life from Lars's apartment.

"Good for you!" my mother said.

"What on earth are you talking about? Take this psychopath, please."

She found a niche for the cage in the back, assured me it had plenty of air pockets, and then climbed into the driver's seat, having already loaded the heavy things.

"Well, we're off!" she said, as if we were going to sea in a schooner, with a piping boatswain and pig-tailed singing seamen, when in fact we were going to her house, with a freaky, self-righteous, red-eyed, greasy-feathered, clapper-clawed parrot in the back of a rented van.

CHAPTER 14

The move home was a turning point for me. Well, less like a turning and more like a case of emergency in which you smash glass. Even with my post-collegiate trickle of bad-paying jobs, I'd never worried that I'd have no place to live. I'd always thought my parents would subsidize my apartment. A year earlier, my sister had gotten herself into such a credit card mess she elected to move home to get her finances in order. How incredible that Adrianna would slide backwards, I'd thought many times, that she would sacrifice the INDEPENDENCE she had earned by agreeing to not only eat meals with my parents, but to share the same bathroom!

I worried about my sister if I made time to think about her at all. She didn't have many friends; her devotion to her job seemed unhealthy; and then there was her weight. "Pleasantly plump," my mother said, if pressed, but my mother was pleasant herself, and my father, who resembled a string bean, claimed judiciously that all of us were "lookers." In high school whenever I had mentioned Adrianna's weight, my parents circled their wagons. "No, we *don't* think teasing strengthens character," they'd say. Adrianna read storybooks to sick children, played F5 and G5 in the handbell ensemble, volunteered at the county board of mental retardation, and won the Latin Club essay contest three years in a row. There was no doubt she was their favorite daughter. Whereas I, the eldest, baffled them because I did not scan the horizon for volunteer opportunities; because I ran from anyone stinking of need; because I hung out at the mall and chased after boys. What was I interested in? Why did I insist on watching TV? How come I didn't apply myself? Was I *really* interested in celebrity beauty secrets or pretending just to rile them?

You can imagine how great it was to jump out of that house at age twenty-one, and now, four years later I was back. As I pulled my banana boxes through the front entrance, past mailbox, mezuzah, and my mother's idea of a whimsical doorknocker (contented pig, antique bronze), past my father's study ("*Per aspera ad astra*," he said, looking up from his stapler), I could hardly believe what was happening to me. My attention snagged on the pencil-marked ladders on the kitchen doorframe, one rung for each daughter's surge of height. Five feet four and a dark lead bar. They thought they had me pegged.

The house hadn't changed since I'd lived there. In the living room there were a few new throw pillows, my father had added to his wardrobe a knit shirt, identical to the one he'd worn the past twenty years, and when I banged around in the kitchen drawers, I invariably turned up some new gizmo. ("What's this?" "Asparagus peeler." "What's this?" "Pineapple slicer." "What's *this*?" "Microplane grater," my mother said, blushing.) But in my bedroom, time had stood still. A child-sized desk contained a sheaf of water-stained notebook paper, three butterscotch candies, a perfectly preserved Chapstick, and two broken hairclips. I trod on the shag rug in which I'd burnt a hole when I was fifteen, flicked on the bedside lamp shaped like a ballerina, and lay on the chenille bedspread, yellow with pink fringe. On the pillows my mother had propped up the old, soft, heart-sickening gang of stuffed animals: Skipper, Frisky, Buttons, My-Mys, Silky Boy, Toodles-Free, Plush . . . Fuck you all, I wanted to say, and hurl them against the wall.

The only new feature of my room was Richard. I had tried to establish his cage in the kitchen, or the living room, or the dining room, but my father sneezed and streamed like there was no tomorrow. So feather dust decided it: Richard lodged with me. "Do I even know for sure he sleeps at night?" I thought our first evening together, the blankets pulled up to my chin. Down the hall, the dishwasher had long ceased rumbling; no cars tore along the road; not even a dog walker tramped by to adorn the silence with a cheery jingle. I listened: no sound. No squawks, no creepy snores, no rustling in the cage. Wildly grateful, I took two Xanax and fell asleep.

As the dawn crept in, Richard began to scream. Scraaaaw! Scraaaww! Scraaaaawww! This became routine. Even on the rare morning when he was quiet, I lay awake, sweating bullets, *waiting* for the screams.

"Darling, just uncover his cage," my mother said. "I think it's his way of saying, Heigh-ho, let's start my morning!"

And it wasn't as if the rest of the house offered peace. Often, under the guise of cooking, my mother monopolized the kitchen for hours, clattering pots and pans, singing along to the music of the swinging forties, and running the garbage disposal. What was she *grinding* in there, I wondered. If I didn't know better, I'd think it was a human carcass. My father, by no stretch of the imagination a talker, nevertheless whistled, stomped, coughed, and called out domestic requests to my mother, which he amplified, against his nature, in order to be heard over her swinging forties. Adrianna was the worst, though. She waylaid me in any room for casual conversation; played computer games that beeped and buzzed; and in the shower, vigorously blew her nose (into a washcloth? Into the water stream itself? Did I *want* to know?). "Well," Adrianna said, "have you heard from Lars?" "I just *left* him." "I know," she said eagerly, "but I thought maybe he'd call." A few days later: "So," Adrianna said. "Any word from Lars?" "I told you, I left him." "Sometimes things drag on."

By the third week, the best thing about living at home, I'd

decided, was the square footage. I don't cherish the ranch house as an architectural form, but my parents' house ran to so many rooms that, in daylight, I could fall into a stride and imagine myself aboard the Hispaniola. I came to think of the kitchen as the galley; and the living room as the main hold; and the long dark coffin of a dining room in which I endured countless suffocating family dinners, I renamed the round-house, not knowing what that meant but liking the idea of its not having any corners. In this way the stale homestead became a vessel of fresh adventure, though once I made the mistake of picking up the phone when Aunt Boothie called and listened to her talk, quite brazenly, about what it meant that both my sister and I were living rent-free in our parents' house.

"Quite frankly I don't think of this as a house," I said.

I have to hand it to my mother. My first week home, she cooked my favorite foods, or what she *remembered* were my favorite foods; her memory had stalled, like a wet engine, at my senior year in high school. She lit candles, broke out the cloth napkins, and tried to pretend that we were celebrating some kind of holiday. What kind of holiday would that be? Take Your Daughter In When Her Boyfriend Kicks Her Out Day? Anyway she tried. She served wine at dinner in hand-blown amethyst-swirled Mexican glasses and smiled wet-eyed as she raised her glass: "How wonderful that we're all together again!" But she didn't have the family behind her. Adrianna sighed heavily, my father looked blank, I scowled, and after a week or so, she gave up the effort. And then, strangest of all, Adrianna started disappearing at night.

"Where does she go?" I asked one evening when my parents and I were scraping leftovers out of the fridge.

"Who?" my father said.

"Adrianna. This is the third dinner she's missed this week. Where is she?"

"I have no idea."

"We don't ask her," my mother said mildly.

I would ask her. I had too much time on my hands *not* to ask her. It wasn't that I thought she was up to anything interesting. She had probably signed up for a night class on how to make a drum out of a gourd. But the fact that she'd do it without telling us was bizarre. Her life was always out in the open. Every scrap, blowing loose like a tissue in the breeze. When I asked her what she had been getting up to in her off-hours, she replied woodenly that she hadn't been up to anything.

"These awkward absences from dinner," I clarified.

"Awkward?"

"You're leaving me a bit exposed. If you're not there to babble on about your day, they're likely to ask *me* questions. I'm not eager for an interrogation, and now I have to manage them without you."

She looked at me blankly. "You don't have to *manage* them. Just talk to them. They're people."

"Mom and Dad? Like hell they are! Anyway don't try to change the subject. Where've you been?"

"Working late," she said, but I didn't believe her. How much prep does a third grade teacher have? One, two, sometimes three times a week, she would leave the house while I was dreaming bad dreams under the yellow chenille spread and not return till after dark.

My mother seemed to know her schedule, but each night, sucker that I was, I counted on her return until the deadly moment when my mother set the table. Three plates? My heart sank. Where was she? The deserter! One night, after deflecting a series of barely-veiled remarks from my mother ("So, Sweetie, I went by the gift wrap department today at Flounkers, and you know who I saw? Your old boss Edie. She says the Christmas rush is already *starting*. I wonder if they could use people."), after eating two extra helpings of lasagna in an effort to maintain a mouth too full to answer my father's questions ("What are the other people in your class doing? The other English majors?"), after voluntarily leaping up to clear the table and wash the dishes just to erect a physical barrier between them and me, I took a strategic position in the kitchen. At 10 P.M. my mother planted a kiss on my cheek as if she were scattering salt onto the drive. "Sleep well," she said blandly. My father had scudded down the hallway without any ceremony.

Listening to the uneven hum of the refrigerator, I tried to read but soon gave up, cut the lights, and waited for the sound of Adrianna's car in the drive. I became one hundred and eighteen pounds of human ear, vibrating with every impulsion of air, every click and creak of the house until, just as the digital clock on the stove said eleven-twenty-eight, her figure loomed in the doorway. She flicked on the light, said, "Oh!" and peeled off her parka to reveal a long brown velour dress—soft, hideous, and intricately embroidered with flowers at the yoke.

"Where've you been?" I said.

"Working."

She threw her coat on a kitchen chair and failed to register my meaningful silence.

"Nobody stays up till midnight doing lesson plans for third graders."

"I do. What's got into you?"

"What's got into *you*?" I parried. "Do you know what you smell like?"

"Jean Naté?"

"No, sister. You smell like sex."

"Gross," she said, ducking as I leaned in to sniff. We engaged in a brief scuffle during which I tried to smell her hair and her hands, but she eluded me, laughing nervously and emitting small unattractive grunts. I was only trying to get a rise out of her, but her reaction suggested I had happened on the correct line of pursuit. Adrianna has a prude's decorum, which she would do anything to preserve, so I stopped chasing her and began to say things she didn't want to hear. She interrupted, she evaded, she tried to shut me up, and then just when I threatened to embarrass her completely—by telling her the details of my *own* sex life—she caved.

"All right, all right. I *wasn't* at work, it's true. I've been *seeing* somebody."

"Who?" I said coolly.

She opened up the refrigerator and pretended to stare at its contents. "Nobody you know," she told the Brita water filter.

"How do you know? I might. I know people. I know more people than *you* know. Maybe I've already dated him."

"You are so competitive, it's sick."

I laughed dryly. "Adrianna, I'm not trying to compete with you."

"You can quit fishing. I'm not going to talk about it." She pushed the refrigerator door shut and stared dully at the photo magnets cluttering its face.

"Well," I said in my most magnanimous manner, "I think it's wonderful news, even if you do carry on like a frantic dog, burying the bone in the yard. I'm sure he's worthy of the mystery. And he signals the end of a long dry spell, am I right? It's not Eddie Wisbey, is it?"

Eddie Wisbey was a short, thick-set guy, red-bearded, who had repeatedly tried to start a contra dance club in high school.

"You think you're so funny," Adrianna said.

"I'm just trying to get my mind around who it could be. Seriously."

"I'm going to bed now."

"Okay. But listen." I touched her elbow lightly. "Lovers

can't hide out forever. I understand," I added gravely, "that you might not want Mom in your business. She can be so . . . well . . . embarrassing . . . and incredibly tactless, but I'm your sister. I'm more like a peer."

"I feel distinctly peerless," Adrianna said.

" . . . So if you should need someone to vet him—you know, an ambassador from the family—I'd be happy to do it, and could do it nicely, without him even knowing I'm there to judge him. I know how to put guys at ease."

Adrianna stared at me, aghast. "Why would I want someone to 'vet' my relationship? Aren't I a grown-up? And aren't romantic relationships *about* trust and intimacy?"

Trust and intimacy? Dear god! Of course, I'd caught the fumes of her psychobabble before. But this would be the moment when a person who actually believed that claptrap would drop the subject or simply leave the room. Instead Adrianna sighed, opened up the refrigerator again, and mechanically began eating mashed potatoes out of a container with her bare fingers. I pressed my advantage.

"My offer wasn't meant to be insulting, Adrianna. Really it's not my fault if you have bad self-esteem. I *wish* I'd had more perspective on Lars's personality early on. If someone I trusted had met him, say, last December, and given me a frank opinion, maybe I never would have moved in with him."

"We all met him. We thought he was nice. Nicer, at times, than you. You're not really saying that if I'd told you to ditch him, you'd have done that? That's crazy! As if you could run your heart by committee . . . "

"I don't want to talk about Lars, that dumb asshole. I want to talk about *your* boyfriend. Come on. I'm your sister. When do I get to meet him?"

"Never."

"At least tell me his name."

"No."

"Why? Give me one good reason."

"Because you have boundary issues. Because you're mean-spirited and unsentimental about other people's affections. Because if young love was a flower growing on your lawn, you would crush it under your heel."

"Jesus. Are you saying you're in *love?*"

"This conversation is over." She licked a dollop of mashed potato off her wrist and lumbered off to bed.

I guess I should have waited. She might have softened in time, and I certainly would have preferred to leave her to pursue her romance in privacy. But her words alarmed me. Two weeks, by my calculations, she had been seeing this guy and now she thought she was in love? And worse, that love was a flower? Given how little experience she had in the domain of personal relationships, I thought it my responsibility to keep an eye on her.

I found my opportunity one Thursday afternoon when Adrianna came home around five o'clock—just to change her clothes, my mother told me; she was going out again.

"Where?"

"I don't ask where," my mother said.

She was in the laundry room (folding, always folding).

"I'm going out too," I said. "Don't be alarmed if I'm not back for dinner."

"In this cold weather?" my mother answered. "You don't have a car. Where are *you* going to go?"

I masked my resentment of her tone and muttered something, admittedly improbable, about fresh air and exercise.

Adrianna was still in her room, scuffing around in her closet, so I had ample time to struggle into my coat and secret myself in the backseat of her surprisingly filthy car. There I lay, perfectly still, resisting the urge to read her crumpled mail or put the caps back on her ballpoints. When the driver's door opened, she slid herself in with a hummmph, and started up the motor, having, thank goodness, taken no notice of me.

I don't know that I've had occasion to mention this, but I don't drive much. I have a license, but I don't like unfamiliar roads, or narrow lanes, or driving at night, or on highways, or in bad weather. Under the best conditions, my heart thumps and my palms drip and don't even get me started on my perineum. Because I prefer anyone but me to do the driving, I pay scant attention to navigation and tend, when it comes to street directions, to be a little vague. Although I know Adrianna drove down Curtis Boulevard, once she took a few quick turns, I was disoriented. I could only see the treetops and couldn't follow the curves the roads were taking. I was completely clueless as to our whereabouts, when a sudden crackle of static made me jump.

A drive-in! Did her boyfriend work here? She gave her hamburger order, and the voice on the intercom answered her without love or undue recognition. We drove to a second drive-in; did her boyfriend work *here*? No, she ordered a Caramel Frappucino and drove on. I had just begun to doubt this adventure when the car came to a halt and she cut the motor. I could tell we were parked in somebody's driveway. She ate the last bite of her burger and tossed the paper bag into the back seat, where it landed on my neck. A long silence—during which she checked her teeth in the rearview mirror—and then she opened her door and plonked herself out. I counted to twenty-five and then followed.

She had led me to a house—a modest two story with sagging windows and yellow aluminum siding. A narrow cement path, adequately shoveled, led to the front door, but I trod on the lawn for fear of alerting Adrianna to my presence. As soon as the snow crunched underfoot I realized, with regret, that I was leaving footprints. But even with this mistake, the cold night air, and the silvery moon in the sky, and the sudden realization that Adrianna could be in danger inside this squat little house, exhilarated me. I ran for an opening in the shrubs and crouched under a curtained window, hoping to hear something. I heard wind. A squirrel fussing in a tree. A neighbor's stereo (Bonnie Raitt, I think). And then, from within that unknown house, I distinctly heard a scream.

There was no time to think. I sprung from my crouch and fell upon the front door, which swung open and immediately plunged me into darkness. I took a few tentative steps and heard sounds—short, weird, panting sounds—as if Adrianna were on the floor getting her throat slit.

"Who's there?" I cried, stumbling forward, palming the wall until I found a switch. The lights blazed on and there was my sister sitting on a man's face.

I knew him. Not right away, of course, but as the tableau dissolved, his face was plain to me. He was the principal of the middle school where my father taught and a friend of my parents. In fact, now that I thought about it, I had been to this house as a kid, once or twice, to trim the tree.

It's shocking and unpleasant to see your sister getting eaten out by anyone, let alone an old man. I screamed; she screamed; I gagged a little; then he, Mr. Tatum, got up, wiping his mouth with his sleeve, and tried to pretend this was the kind of situation where people can look each other in the eye.

"Did you *follow* me here?" Adrianna said. Then—I forget her exact words—she called me a stalker and said some more in that melodramatic vein. Mr. Tatum tried to calm her down.

"Is something wrong?" he asked. "Everything all right with your folks?"

My parents' health was everything we would wish it to be, I admitted.

"Then why are you here?" Adrianna said.

"Because I thought you said you had a *boy*friend. And I wanted to make sure you weren't in over your head or needlessly debasing yourself."

"Shut up," she said. "I am not debasing myself!"

"But Adrianna!" Obviously it was an effort not to say terribly rude things about Mr. Tatum as he stood right there, fussing with his belt buckle, but I did my best. I alluded to him not by name. I called their relationship 'this.' As in "*This* is a terrible mistake. *This* is one of those instances where you're confusing age with experience. Maybe *this* is something you ought to discuss with a licensed therapist." Here she clearly took offense, but in an effort to keep things civilized she said, "Well, *that's* the pot calling the kettle black." "Well, don't you think *the old grey mare* just ain't what she used to be?" And so on and so on, strangling our points in a hideous macramé of clichés. I wouldn't judge a book by its cover. I'm not judging the book by its cover, I'm just saying all that glitters is not gold. If you can't stand the heat, get out of the kitchen. I had only cried, "Don't blame the messenger," when Adrianna grabbed a Lucite paperweight from the coffee table. "Somebody has to *send* for a messenger," she howled.

"Ladies!" said Mr. Tatum.

There were no ladies present—it was an imaginary appeal—but it got her to put the paperweight down. They had a brief struggle themselves, which involved an embarrassing number of clutches and endearments I tried not to witness, and then Adrianna tore out of the house and drove off before I could explain—especially that she was my ride.

Mr. Tatum looked at me with quiet dismay.

"Do you want to sit down?" he said.

"Not where she was sitting."

I was aiming to lighten the tense situation, but he didn't get it. He was *so old*.

"You've had a shock. Why don't you sit down on the Chesterfield?" He indicated a high-backed leather sofa, tufted and cracked. "I'll get you some water."

Once he had passed me the green rippled Depression glass, he began: "It's not what you think . . . "

"You don't know what I think, Mr. Tatum."

He raised a purple-veined, age-spotted hand. "Please. I've known you forever. Call me Don."

"And I've known you," I scoffed, "since you were fifty." I sat with my arms folded, ankles crossed. "Where is Mrs. Tatum right now? Tutoring refugees? Shopping for Christmas presents? Taking your grandchildren to dinner?"

"My wife died eight years ago," he said softly. "I believe you came to the funeral."

"Did I?" Oh god. There rose a dim memory of being dragged to a funeral parlor for some lady's untimely demise, a vague recollection of a woman who had somehow seemed to die of her femaleness. I couldn't recall the details, but I wasn't about to be disarmed by pity, so I expressed my condolences to Mr. Tatum swiftly, and then reminded him that this match with my sister was hardly what anyone in my family might have hoped for. The fact that he and Adrianna were carrying on in secrecy indicated that he already knew as much.

He answered my objections in the blustery pseudo-sophisticated way you'd expect. A matter of privacy, not secrecy. Two consensual adults. An unexpected and noisy bit of sunshine in his quiet not to say cloudy life. Once I took a moment to collect myself and understand the facts, I might even discover I wanted to apologize for my intrusion. I imagine this is how he spoke to the delinquent adolescents he met in his office: reasonable, slightly disappointed, even-handed, with a note of self-pity, convincing you that he was the wronged party.

"Mr. Tatum, are your hands shaking right now because you're nervous, or because you're old?"

He withdrew his hands, in surprise, and folded them in his lap. "My dear, I do think you're over-reacting. Your sister isn't underage."

"No, but she's under-used. She's never had a boyfriend. Has she told you that?"

He smiled indulgently and tsk-tsked me. "You always *were* the provocative one."

"I was the good-looking one, if you want to know the truth, and I don't like your thinking you can mess around with Adrianna just because she's the ugly duckling."

He looked taken aback. "You underestimate your sister, surely. She is anything but ugly." He rose to indicate our interview was over. "I think you should have the rest of this conversation with Adrianna."

"Fine. But I don't have a way home."

"How did you get here?"

And then that old embarrassing conversation. You didn't drive? No, didn't drive. Don't you drive? Well, yes, can drive, but don't have a car. No car? Well, phobic about driving. "All right," he said icily. "I'll drive you home."

That was a fun ride.

CHAPTER 15

Adrianna didn't talk to me for two weeks. In the absence of her explanations, I began to consider her "love affair" in new lights. Maybe, I reasoned, she was sitting on his face for monetary reasons. Maybe she let him do things to her in exchange for cash, with a long-term plan to pay off her credit card debt and move out of our parents' house. And yet, however hard I tried to imagine Adrianna as a player—someone who would trade sexual favors for cash—I stumbled on her basic goodness. She had spoken of love as a flower that might be crushed underfoot. More likely she thought she loved Mr. Tatum and was oblivious to how large a role his financial steadiness played in the attraction. I once used the term "Sugar Daddy" in her presence and she missed my meaning entirely, recalling instead, with childish enthusiasm, the milk caramel lollipop of the same name.

Still I needed to understand the contours of this affair. How long had she been seeing Mr. Tatum? Was she seeing only him or might there be other old unattractive men involved? To answer these questions I ventured into her room when she was at work. I was looking for a diary; instead I found a batch of letters. Pathetic things! She had wrapped them up in a gold ribbon from a chocolate box and hidden them under her mattress. Reader, you can imagine what an old man writes a young woman when he thinks nobody else is going to read the dreck. *Last night was unforgettable* (and then tedious quasi-poetic, quasi-porno reminders of what he couldn't forget). Foreign-language endearments: *mi muñeca, mon petit canard en plastique*. Places he wanted to take her, show her, touch her, et cetera. His penmanship was all right, but he probably wrote the letters wearing his best bifocals. Was it my imagination, or did the very pages smell of milk of magnesia, glycerine soap? Adrianna hadn't arranged the letters in chronological order, but gradually I began to make out an emotional pattern. On the left hand of the desk, I placed the booty letters: Thank you for last night, You are so lovely I hardly believe I deserve you, et cetera. On the right hand of the desk, pleas and promises: Give me time, Tell me what I did wrong, I know I can make it up to you, et cetera. And in the chaotic middle, everything else: a photocopied Shakespearean sonnet (the one about "bare ruined choirs," for *obvious* reasons); the lyrics to "Ain't Misbehavin'"; and a memo from The Board of Education about school lunches regarding the importance of incorporating whole grains.

I *thought* I was interested in playing detective, but by the third encomium to a salty pair of Adrianna's underwear, I couldn't bear to read another word, let alone arrange the letters in order and figure out the dates.

I knew enough already: the affair was farther along than I'd even feared.

"Mom, do you know who Adrianna is seeing at nights?"

"Oh, *is* she seeing someone?" My mother looked up from the apples she was coring on a medieval-looking appliance she had clamped to the counter.

"Someone you know. Don't you want to ask her?"

"If she wants to tell us, she'll tell us."

"'When she's ready,'" I mocked.

"Exactly!"

That's the thing with liberal parents. Proud of their so-called respect for boundaries, they averted their gazes while we stepped in the dog shit. Did they have curiosity? If they knew their youngest daughter was fucking an old family friend, would they care? Maybe they wouldn't. Maybe they'd say, Well, I'm sure if it's not a match made in heaven, she'll figure it out for herself. "We've always believed in letting our children find their own way," I can hear my mother saying.

I'm sorry to say that despite the shocking discovery of Adrianna's affair, things carried on much as usual. Adrianna avoided my company, and I kept her secret, annoyed as hell, but confident that its value might appreciate in time. I got used to a certain companionable rhythm with my mother, who divided her time between cooking, laundry, housework, water aerobics, dance lessons, trips to Costco and Wild Birds Unlimited, and tutoring Latin stragglers. On weekends my father and Adrianna fell upon us, boring us with their lesson plans, scrounging through the kitchen, watching TV. Some nights all four of us would eat together and then sit in the main hold to watch *Moulin Rouge* or whatever was on television; other nights I would eat with my parents alone, imagining Mr. Tatum eating Adrianna. Then my mother would get out the classifieds and in her discreet way try to excite me about future employment.

"All right, *here's* one."

"One what?"

"CROWDED CLOSET. Experience with sales. Ask for Doug."

"I'm not interested in retail. Especially a thrift store. Dead people's clothes and other people's cast-offs? I'll stay in my *own* closet, thanks."

"Which reminds me," my mother said. "I did some reorganizing for you. Just went through and pulled out *very* worn things, your hoodie from high school, the drama T-shirts, old socks with holes." I nodded. She read on:

Want a job that will "MEAT" [she spelled this out and winked before continuing] your expectations? Local grocery needs MEAT CUTTER.
HOUSEHOLD HELP. Fun loving family of 6 needs help keep-

ing home running smoothly. Please have superb laundry skills, including washing, ironing and mending.

THE PRETZEL PLACE looking for upbeat, high energy people to fill counter positions. Apply at mall location.

"You like soft pretzels," my mother added, eyebrows raised.

"Leave me alone," I said. "If you want to work on someone's problems, look to your *other* daughter." But she never took my hints.

CHAPTER 16

Richard was molting, and scruffy as he was, there was something enviable in his ability to start fresh. I opened my book, but couldn't read a line. The room felt stuffy and hot. "It's big, it's hot, it's back!" Richard said, dragging out a chewed feather.

After further thought, I took the bright green feather to Adrianna's room.

"Want a bookmark?" I said, holding it aloft. She closed the door.

I tried reading in the living room, but my father had the TV on loud enough to reach the Dry Tortugas. In the kitchen, my mother scraped carrots and listened to *The Fabulous Danny Boy Album*: one song; twelve artistic interpretations.

"How long am I to lie here in this old berth?" I said, slumping on the breakfast bar.

"Are you sick?" my mother said.

"No."

"It's cabin fever then." She stopped scraping carrots. In a minute she had found her purse, tucked a few bills into my hand, and advised me to get out of the house. The weather was miserable, but off I went. I tramped a few blocks, pretending to enjoy the open air, before making a beeline for a shopping center, where I found a newly opened sandwich shop.

A small and predominantly plastic place, the shop boasted a service counter, three booths sticky enough to discourage loitering, and a vinyl menu board with changeable white letters, most of which spelled something fatally wrong (i.e. "wheat, white, onion role, or rye"). Not the sort of place I would go twice. But as fate would have it, I knew the girl behind the counter—a plump person with one blue eye and one green eye. One glance at her and I seemed to have dropped to all fours and was tunneling deep into the past.

"Patty Pacholewski! What are you doing here? This is a stunning stroke of luck."

"Do I know you?" the broad-shouldered girl said, wiping her hands on her apron.

"Mrs. Buskirk's class! Fifth grade, and beyond. Don't you remember?"

Once she recovered from the surprise, we fell into easy and affable conversation, reminiscing about the afternoons I had spent at her house (she lived in a carriage house by a lake, with a glamorous spiral staircase, and a mother who descended from it, scowling). I asked how was her little brother (fine), and her dog (dead), and her mother and father (fine and dead, respectively), and she asked why I had been so mean to her in seventh grade, to which I had no answer. I ordered turkey bacon and tomato, but what I really wanted to know was did she remember reading *Treasure Island* and how all us girls had sat with our hands below desk level, passing around her bracelets and rings.

"No, but I kind of remember my rings."

"Your jewelry never looked like it came from a bubblegum machine," I said with admiration.

"You drew pictures of it, do you remember? You had a notebook and you made an inventory of all the girls in the class and their clothes."

"No," I said, marveling. "But that sounds like me."

I recalled how Long John Silver says to Jim Hawkins, "You're a noticing kind of person." A lot of times I'll be out for a walk and somebody will point out something that escaped me: sky seems hazy, crocuses in bloom, just passed a burrow which belongs to some kind of small animal, your guess is better than mine. Since the break-up with Lars, I had been worried that I was *not* a noticing person, but of course, I am; I just notice different things.

"Who?" my mother was saying to me a few hours later, as she bent over and stuck her head into the dryer. "This lint trap is eating our towels. No, I don't remember. Well, the name sounds familiar. One of your elementary school friends?"

"Honestly, Mom. How could you not remember? Patty Pacholewski was a deity in fifth grade."

I pushed aside an empty basket and sat down on the counter, thinking about Patty. How we had shared her heart-shaped bangles, her dolphin rings. Her puffy-sleeved, round-collared, pastel-colored blouses. The holiday concert to which she wore a blouse of slippery, white sateen. Her charm bracelet with a heart toggle clasp, my own parrot green windbreaker whose white hood ties I had chewed to a pulp, her pale pink car coat made of light brushed wool which hung on the peg in the cloak room three pegs down from mine. And her umbrella! Also pink, with a white handle in the shape of a swan.

"I used to move my desk around the classroom, to get a better view of her blue eye or a better view of her green one."

"Was she the diabetic?"

"No, that was Johanna Miller," I said testily.

"Sweetheart." My mother dropped a dark globe of lint into the trashcan and turned to me with an openly worried face. "Did you feed Richard today? When I went in your room to get your clothes, he looked lackluster. I took him the left-over tabbouli."

"Okay, whatever."

"Darling, a bird is a responsibility. You have to feed him *every* day, not just when you feel like it." Insert lecture on nutrition here. "Your father thinks he needs exercise."

When my mother first mentioned Richard, the sternness of her gaze had given me a pang; I felt like Jim Hawkins, pinned by a knife to the mast. But now I started to laugh. "Daddy *said* that?"

"You *know* how he is. Why are you laughing?"

"No reason."

But later I marched into Adrianna's room and said, "How many times has Mom pulled you aside, and told you in a calculatedly casual way, 'Your father feels this,' 'What's important to your father is that'?"

"I thought we weren't talking."

"Oh, let's give that up," I said. "I'm sorry if I barged in on you on top of old Smokey, but when I followed you to his house, I didn't know what I was going to see. Anyway, I haven't told Mom and Dad. So your secret is safe with me."

She regarded me warily. Lately her "dates" had been a bit erratic and there had been some late night muffled phone calls. I'd gathered the affair wasn't going all that well, but had strategically made a point of not prying. Now I lay down on the rug of her room and gently guided my legs over the back of my head. "If you can't afford the healings," Bev had said, "take up something you *can* afford," and she had demonstrated, quite powerfully, a yoga maneuver called "the plough." I often did the plough while reading *Treasure Island*, but it made my neck hurt.

"Anyway," I panted, "you do know what I mean about Mom. It's like she radios into headquarters for Dad's feelings, when she senses hers need backup." I lowered my legs back to the rug and exhaled.

"You need a job," Adrianna said. "You need a wider perspective on life and a wider range of interests."

"A materialist way of looking at things. Right now I'm on a spiritual journey and not so naïve to think a job is going to solve my problems. When the log-house fills with smoke, and Jim Hawkins and the crew think they're trapped, the captain cries, 'Out, lads, out, and fight 'em in the open!' So Jim grabs a cutlass."

"I'm afraid the opportunities for brandishing a cutlass have long passed," Adrianna said. "I've been fighting with Don," she added abruptly.

Apparently when I had been at pains to share a crucial incident in a life-changing novel, she had given her mind permission to wander, and it had wandered right into the cul-de-sac of her sorry-ass relationship. I couldn't pretend to be surprised, but I did pretend briefly not to know who she was talking about. Her need to confide was so great that she let my jibe pass.

"Not exactly fighting," she said. "But things have been a little rough lately. It's absolutely baffling . . . "

"I thought you guys were so in love."

"Well, we are," she said, deaf to sarcasm. "Our feelings for each other are as strong as ever. Really, I couldn't ask for a better man than Don." Here I had to be careful not to gag. "But we're struggling over little things," she went on. "And I'm getting tired of having to reassure him all the time about his age."

"Oh, is he feeling . . . elderly?"

"I tell him I don't care; I like that he's mature and knows his mind, but he says I don't know what I'm missing. He worries that he's depriving me of a more exciting dating life."

"It's true you haven't played the field much."

"I don't want to play the field!" She shook her head. "Actually I think the problem is that his father is sick, and his mother, who's a few years younger, is exhausted by taking care of him, and he looks at them having a hard time, and imagines how we could turn out."

"His parents are still alive? They must be ancient!"

"People live a long time now, you know."

"There's not much about love in *Treasure Island*. If you'd read it, you'd find it more of a study of friendships between men. I suppose that's why I find it so liberating. I've had enough of romances where the woman exhausts herself, just pouring herself into her man, obsessing about his comings and goings."

Just then the laptop sitting on her desk bleeped. She had mail. "It's probably from *him*," she said. "Do you mind? I want to read it alone."

"Not at all," I said, getting up to leave. "But I thought you guys only did snail mail."

"What made you think that?"

Here, I am embarrassed to say, I let my gaze wander to her mattress, under which she stored her horrid collection of billet-doux. She followed my gaze and blushed deeply.

"Get out of my room," she said in a trembling voice. "Now!"

The next time I checked under the mattress, the beribboned stash was gone. I could have found it, I'm sure, but I had better things to do than tear her room apart. By now I had studied *Treasure Island* to a nicety and the studies were paying off. I could stand in line at the sandwich shop and riff on one or two Core Values before Patty had even rung my order up.

"Where was I?" I said as she knocked a roll of quarters against the register's edge. "Oh yeah, so now I've rid myself of a terrible job, and a terrible boyfriend, I'm free to direct my life in ways I'd never imagined. Did I ever tell you how I met Lars? I didn't seize on him as a boyfriend; I didn't pluck him from a field of guys. I drifted into the thing like so much driftwood, do you know what I mean? When do you see Jim Hawkins drifting into anything? Everything he does—thank you, but I think you still owe me a nickel—everything he does, is because he gets an idea in his head. Patty, *you* should read *Treasure Island*. You're kind of dawdling in the harbor, right, what with this sandwich shop job. I bet if you read thirty pages, you'd lift up anchor and sail into the open sea towards your goal!"

"I have a goal," Patty said, "and that's to get through my shift with as little human interaction as possible."

She was a laugh, that Patty!

Truthfully, I'm the kind of person who throws things away—letters, photos, tiresome clothes and people—and finding Patty was like finding some old thing in the closet that I had *meant* to discard. First there is annoyance ("I thought I'd thrown this out"), then the dawning realization of your luck. Once I threw away a curling iron and wore my hair straight for twelve weeks. Just when I was ready to go curly again, I found the iron under a silk camisole I'd never washed. There was a kind of fate in it. The indicator light no longer worked, but it was basically all right.

Patty was a great find. In some ways I was more sentimental about her girlhood than my own. She was the only girl whose hair had appeared in a new shape each day: braids, plaits, buns, banana-like funnels. She was the only girl who had worn creased navy slacks and pale colored blouses. Even now, in her sandwich shop blouse, which I knew was not of her choosing, and a visor, which dulled a bit the shine of her hair, she sent my mind flying back to years of kaleidoscopic detail, a time when a fresh pair of rainbow shoelaces or a polka-dot ribbon on a barrette felt, to a girl, like the revolution of a planet. And she was always calling up memories, whether she meant to or not. Once when I complained that she had stinted me on garnishes, she slapped on a few more pickles. "I don't care how many pickles you have. They're not *my* pickles," she said and suddenly I sang:

My mother and your mother live across the way.
Every night they have a fight and this is what they say:
Icky bicky pickle pie,
Icky bicky boo.
Icky bicky pickle pie,
Out goes you!

"The jump rope rhyme, remember?" I said. "Enid Crawley and I used to do it all the time."

"Enid Crawley got pregnant in eleventh grade."

"No kidding! And she was the best at Double Dutch. I *did* run into her at the mall last year, and she looked about a hundred years old. I'm glad *we* didn't get knocked up. I mean, I assume you didn't get knocked up."

"No," she said, rubbing a non-existent stain on the counter. "But I did have an abortion our senior year."

"No kidding! Patty, I didn't even know you'd been sexually active. Excuse me for being forward, but since I rediscovered this book, my whole life has been about being forward." Knowing what my mouth was about to say, my left leg began to spasm. I leaned more heavily onto the counter. "I've told you about the Core Values, right?"

"Yeah, you wrote them on one of our comment cards last week."

"So do you know what I mean when I say I can't blow my own horn right now? This winter has felt like a huge setback. I'm BOLD, as you know, I'm RESOLUTE, but I'm definitely falling short in the INDEPENDENCE arena. I mean, I can't live at my parents' house another moment if I'm going to keep evolving. My sister lives at home too, but—did I tell you this already?—she's having a creepy affair with a much older man."

"I was only seventeen. It was horrible."

"What? Patty, have you heard a word I'm saying?"

She stared right at me: "You need a place to crash."

"Yes, exactly! Do you live alone?"

"No, I live with my girlfriend."

I didn't know what she meant by that. "You have TWO bedrooms?"

"Three, actually."

"Then you have extra space!"

"Not exactly." Attempting an emphatic gesture, she

knocked over a stack of Styrofoam cups, which rolled across the counter.

"I don't put much faith in your math skills," I said as she pursued a cup approaching the edge. "You live with ONE girl-friend, but your apartment has THREE bedrooms."

"Yeah, but one of them is sort of our media room . . . "

"Less TV, more reading. I recommend it. And I'd even sleep in the living room, or a sun porch, if you have that. Jim Hawkins sleeps in an apple barrel. Anyway, this is excellent! Roommates with Patty Pacholewski! In fifth grade, I never would have thought it." (Seventh grade, I wouldn't have wanted to think it, but didn't say.) "Tell me the truth, Patty: would you have asked me, if I hadn't asked you first?"

"Did you ask me?" All the color had gone out of her face. Her day job sucked the life out of her. "You don't even know my girlfriend, Sabrina."

"But I'd love to know her."

"Listen, I really have to go fill the napkin dispensers now—no offense."

"None taken, mate! You, me and Sabrina—let's find a time!"

Thank god for Patty Pacholewski, I thought as I walked home, kicking at snow boulders, many of which shattered violently at the first touch of my boot. When, I wondered idly, had *she* become a lesbian?

Back at the ranch, I discovered that someone had placed a letter into Chapter 1: The Old Sea Dog at the 'Admiral Benbow.'

"What's this?" I said.

"That came for you yesterday," my mother said. "I wanted to make sure you'd see it."

The note was from Rena on a fine hand-made rice paper embedded with marigold petals. I read it rapidly; it was plain she was worked up.

. . . I miss the Gratuitous Pancakes. Why do all my calls go straight to voicemail? Are you mad that I took your shift at The Pet Library? Please write back. XOXO, Big Love, Rena

I ignored the letter. I had Patty now.

"Rena called," my mother said.

"Rena called," Adrianna said.

"Somebody's on the phone for you," my father said. "Her name's Rowena."

Eventually Adrianna chased me down, phone in hand. "She's right here," she told the receiver in a loud, aggrieved voice.

"Yes?" I said (politely, almost secretarial).

"What's happening? Do you want to get a cup of coffee? How's Richard, how's living at home?"

"A hundred questions at once!" But I regretted my sharpness. What if the Patty situation didn't pan out? Crashing with Rena would be a retreat to primordial self without the boon of my mother's well-stocked pantry, but it would do to keep my options open. "Sorry, Rena, don't mean to be blunt. I'm just in such a rush."

"Why?"

"Meeting someone."

"Lars?"

"No," I said with a snorting laugh. "Lars means nothing to me now. He's like a bad dream. A distant vapor. I can't even remember the color of his eyes."

"Green," she said.

"He's like a bank of fog that hung over everything and then the moon came up and burned him into nothing. What did I ever see in him?"

"I don't know," she said with just the slightest tremor in her voice. "Green . . . with little gold tiger flecks."

"Wait, first my crappy job, now my crappy boyfriend? Rena, you wouldn't dare!"

"I didn't do anything," she pleaded. "But he was lonely, and I've been missing you. We didn't do *anything*, I swear. I wanted to sound you out first."

"Sound this, you treacherous dog," I said and hung up.

Lying on my crumb-laden bed, I thumbed through *Treasure Island* in search of solace, but the words blurred together, and I threw my book to the floor. Over the last few nights I had been pretending not to hear Adrianna making sad noises in her bedroom. She had been having long talks with Mr. Tatum and taking steamy baths at night, during which I was pretty sure I could detect, under the sounds of splashing, her sobbing. The girlish misery in this house was rising like a sea tide. Squelch it, I thought. I deliberately made myself think of Lars as a compendium of flaws and inadequacies. I remembered his lack of ambition and his habit of smudging his glasses. I remembered his boyishly servile way with my parents (until my mother had finally put a stop to it, he'd called them "ma'am" and "sir") and his piercing, bed-shaking sneezes. I remembered his clothing—all of it, bad; in fact, the best you could say is some was neutral in color—and his penchant for supernatural sci-fi movies. By boarding the brig of his unappealing qualities, I managed to calm myself. Then I picked up my book, thrust it under my pillow, and slept.

When I awoke at dawn, I had an angry red crease on my right cheek where the spine had pressed. No cucumber slices, I vowed, no lotion. The book had cut me like a saber.

BOLDNESS
RESOLUTION
INDEPENDENCE

I didn't care that I couldn't remember the fourth one. Let the rude mark lie. On my way to breakfast, I did a capital imitation of a seaward whistle.

CHAPTER 17

Patty's girlfriend Sabrina sat cross-legged on the floor, in a dark grey smock and cargo pants, smoking. I liked her *instantly*, even though her tattoo alarmed me: a mermaid stabbing herself with Neptune's fork. Patty had gone out for more cigarettes.

"Stephen King," she said, when I asked her what she liked to read. "*Road and Track*, the magazine."

There was a long pause in which she drank her beer, and I drank my water, both of us gazing at Richard, whose cage I had placed on the floor.

"Nice bird," she said at last.

"Thank you. He's supposed to be a helpmate, but he's more of a talisman for my journey towards bolder selfhood. I got him after I read *Treasure Island*."

"Okay," Sabrina said.

Richard rocked from side to side, pupils slightly dilated. He bobbed on his perch in the dance style of Shirley Temple.

"Is he going to talk?" Sabrina asked.

"No, that dance always wears him out. He'll take a nap soon."

He would. I'd given him a piece of Xanax. Although etiquette required me to disclose to Patty and Sabrina that I had a pet, I hadn't wanted to showcase his irritating qualities.

I explained to Sabrina that I knew Patty from fifth grade, and she explained to me that she had grown up in Michigan but at fourteen had run away from home. She had lived on the streets, then in the back of somebody's truck; she had moved here and taken a job fixing motorcycles, which she quit abruptly it seems, or maybe it was just her manner of telling it; then she went back to a different school; dropped out; rode around the country a bit; worked in a fish cannery in Alaska, and before she met Patty I don't know where she lived, though she spoke repeatedly of a drug-dealing person who went by the name of Midas, both because he was regarded as a king of sorts among his peers and because he liked to wear gold chains.

I could not hide a sense of awe. "When Patty first said she had a roommate, I assumed she meant some boring person we both knew in high school."

"I barely attended high school," she said cheerfully.

They lives rough, and they risk swinging, but they eat and drink like fighting-cocks . . . I seen a thing or two at sea, I have.

"What do you do now?" I asked Sabrina. "Odd jobs?"

"Bad jobs, odd jobs, shit jobs. Dishwasher, house painter, deckhand."

"Deckhand," I murmured and mentally gave Sabrina a tarry pigtail.

"Riverboat casino. The people suck, but those jobs are easy to get, if you're looking."

"I haven't been on a boat since I was seven, at Disneyworld. It's A Small World After All."

"That's a *flume* ride, not a boat."

"Well, technically, but I didn't take to it. The colored lights, the dark tunnel, the dolls that sing; even if you close your eyes, their teeny tiny voices bore into your ears. I hurled on the fiberglass deck and had to be evacuated at an emergency exit platform. I never stepped in a boat again."

Sabrina took a slug of beer.

"But people change," I added.

"Not that much," Sabrina said.

"No, that's what's so inspiring about people. People *change*."

She looked skeptical, but we didn't get into it, because just then a snow-flecked Patty walked through the door in a long wool coat. She pulled off her wet boots and gazed at us, almost in disbelief.

"You came?"

"She came and she brought stuff," Sabrina told Patty.

"To new beginnings," I said as I presented them a double-handled shopping bag, which they rifled through with enthusiasm. Pine nuts, sun-dried tomatoes, five-pound bags of Jolly Ranchers. "There's always more where that came from." I ignored the vision of my mother in the empty pantry, steeling herself for another Costco run.

When two women live together they create a world of gestures—flicking of hair, twitching of lips—which make their approval of you seem to hang in the balance. As Sabrina and Patty rummaged through the herbal selection in the mahogany tea chest, I watched them closely. I assumed a relaxed posture on the floor (my hosts having occupied the futon) and tried not to look at Richard, who, pupils further dilated, had started to daven. Sabrina put some throaty folk music on the stereo, and Richard screamed, "It's big, it's hot, it's back!"

"Wow," Patty said.

"He *is* a talker!" Sabrina said with elation.

"So how'd you guys meet?" I said abruptly.

"Softball team," said Patty. "Internet," said Sabrina.

Since they had overlapped, I pretended not to have heard Sabrina and feigned an interest in softball. The conversation tottered along, with intermittent shrieks from Richard.

"Bird's getting lively," Sabrina said.

"Shut the fuck up!" said Richard.

"Sorry. Sorry! I don't know where he—"

"It's big, it's hot, it's back!" shrieked Richard.

"So the extra room?" I put in hurriedly.

"Right now we use the space—I mean it's kind of conven-ient for storage and TV watching—"

"Can't you watch TV in the living room? Because you'd hardly notice me. I'm very considerate, I'm independent . . . "

"How much can you pay?" Sabrina interrupted.

The free gifts from Costco, the peanut butter pretzels that they had already ripped open and were snacking on, for god-sakes, how much of me did they want?

"I can contribute, obviously. Are you open to a barter econ-omy?"

"Not really," Sabrina said, her mouth full of pretzels. "'What does a lesbian bring to a second date?'" She gave Patty a private, almost misty look.

"'A U-Haul,'" Patty replied.

"Old joke," Sabrina explained, looking over at me.

"She *knows* you're not a lesbian," Patty clarified.

"*Are* you a lesbian?" Sabrina asked.

"I'm very homosocial," I said, dredging up a word from college.

"Steer the boat, girlfriend!" screamed Richard.

"Go, bird, go!" Sabrina said.

"I'm celibate," I added.

"It's weird," Patty replied sharply. "You always talk a big game about your ex-boyfriend, but you seem kind of—"

"Book-centered?"

"No." She frowned. "I don't know. Intense."

"Shut up!" Richard said.

"This one's a hoot!" Sabrina said. "Can we feed him?"

Richard edged over to the bars and took a pretzel out of Sabrina's hand, but half-heartedly, I thought, and with half an eye on the chocolate-covered Bing cherries Patty had torn open. There followed a great to-do in which Sabrina and Patty took turns feeding Richard rice cakes, pink Himalayan salt, ice cubes, and a pencil. Each time Richard plucked an object out of their hands, they laughed like fools. Which gave me an idea . . .

"It's a shame I can't touch *his* money," I said, almost to myself. "But his earnings are all tied up in a trust fund."

"Whose money?" Sabrina said.

"Richard. Didn't I tell you? He performs."

"The *bird's* got a trust fund?" Patty said. "What does he do?"

"TV mostly."

Sabrina stared at Richard as if she were mentally rearranging his feathers. "I *thought* he looked familiar."

"Maybe you've seen his commercials."

"Is he the one who can open beer bottles?"

"Oh yeah!" Patty said. "He rides a scooter on late-night talk shows?"

I indicated that his was a vast scroll of talents, still unfolding.

"He's done pizza, toilet paper, peanut butter, Carpet Barn, House of Tan . . . " It was surprisingly easy to make stuff up, like that moment when Jim Hawkins realizes he can paddle off and cut the schooner loose. *One cut with my sea-gully, and the Hispaniola would go humming down the tide!* I cut the ropes and Richard drifted into celebrity. "Did you see the movie that won Best Picture at Sundance last year?"

"No."

"Richard *was* that movie!" I cried.

It was extraordinary how well they received that news, given the impression they gave of not following independent film. Soon all three of us were chatting about animal movies and the best cat and dog commercials we had seen on TV.

"Look, here's what I'll do," I said after a pause calculated to suggest some internal struggle. "If I can stay here, I'll keep Richard's cage in the living room. I'll guarantee you intimate access."

"Really?" Sabrina said.

Patty looked a little doubtful. "But isn't he out working half the time?"

"No way." I explained that he'd just come off a time-consuming shoot and was going on hiatus. He always went on hiatus while molting, I added.

"Could we take him out of the cage?"

"Sure."

"Could we use him at parties?"

"I'll even waive his fee."

"It's big, it's hot, it's back!" Richard said and then he said it a few more times, with some meager variations in pitch.

Sabrina applauded. I was glad to score a point, but I knew the narrowness of my corner. The free association, the feather plucking, the loose bowel movements, could start any minute. I stood to signal my readiness to go.

"Talk it over," I said in an offhand tone. "Let me know."

They stroked the top of Richard's head. They'd pretend to talk it over; I'd go home and pack tonight. Little Richard was going to save me, I thought, but just then, while they tickled his feet one last time, another sound came from his beak.

At first it seemed like a laugh. Then the laugh sort of fell down the stairs and became a wail. That intractable bird, that bird in whom I could barely wedge a useful phrase, had been studying my misery when I'd thought he was asleep. I threw the cloth over his cage and my hands began to tremble. The sound was terrible: defeated, despairing, almost crazy. Shut up, shut up, but he carried on sobbing, relentless as a wave.

"Freaky," Sabrina said. "He cries like a girl."

"He's studying for a heart-breaking dramatic role," I said.

CHAPTER 18

I loathe you," I told Richard. "Don't flap. Don't grind your beak. Don't speak. The cloth means darkness. Night hath fallen. Would that it fell forever on your paltry, coarse, double-crossing soul."

"Have a nice time?" my mother said from the laundry room, where I'd gone to get a damp bath towel to fling on top of his cage—for emphasis.

In the kitchen Adrianna and my father were seated at the breakfast bar, spooning applesauce from a large ceramic dish. My mother followed me in and asked if I wanted some applesauce. No, I said, the firmness of my tone a warning, but my mother pressed on: Sure I didn't want some applesauce? Did I know she'd made the applesauce with cinnamon and vanilla? Was it Adrianna who had always liked it, or was it me? Which one of us had always liked the applesauce? Well, we all had liked the applesauce, hadn't we—

"For god's sake, no applesauce!" I snapped so sharply that my mother's eyes pooled with tears.

"What the heck is *your* problem?" Adrianna said.

"Nothing," I grumbled.

"I mean, jeez, if you don't want to talk, get out of the kitchen."

"Jeez, heck," I jeered.

"If you can't *stand the heat*, get out of the kitchen," my father corrected.

"I'm not speaking idiomatically," Adrianna said.

"It's all right," my mother said. "I wasn't offended. Really."

"This is about courtesy," Adrianna insisted.

Which happens not to be a Core Value, I reminded her, though recently I had displayed courtesy as I affected not to notice all the incredibly annoying things that went on around me. For instance, I hadn't said anything about the fact that Dad stunk up the bathroom, or that my mother's bread rolls were frozen even after she defrosted them, or the fact that she, Adrianna, had been keeping me up half the night with her sobbing.

Diversion accomplished.

My mother turned to her favorite daughter. "Is this true?"

"No."

"Have you been crying?"

Adrianna flushed. "Oh, god. No. I mean, maybe I had one rough night, but hardly . . . "

"Sweetheart, what's upsetting you?" My mother took Adrianna's face in her hands.

"Nothing! Don't you see?" Adrianna squealed. "She's trying to shift the focus!"

"Honey, if you're depressed, your father and I want to know about it."

Your father and I. I laughed out loud; she was radioing in for backup. I swiveled to look at my father who, sure enough, sat placidly eating applesauce, showing no signs of having engaged with Adrianna or her "crisis."

"You can tell us anything," my mother said.

"Do you want me to clear the air, Adrianna?" I asked.

"No."

"Clear the air about what?" my mother said.

Have I said that I *live* for the plain speaking of *Treasure Island*? When I think of all the interference, subtext, and evasion of my childhood, I want to scream and pull the antimacassars off the furniture—and never mind the oily blots on the back of the chair. It was time for someone to tell our parents the truth, I told Adrianna, thinking of how Jim Hawkins speaks the truth to Silver, even at the risk of offense. It could either be her or me, I said, but the fact was she had been drifting around in a leaky ship for days, with no sight of landing.

"Shut up, shut up, shut up!" Adrianna cried.

"Darling, what's wrong?" my mother said.

"Why does she have to talk like that? Why do we *put up* with her talking like that? I know she'll try to make this conversation be about me, but if anything, we should be talking about why she's wrecking *her* life!"

"You girls are always so melodramatic," my mother said.

"She quit work and responsibility and civility just so she can wallow in an escapist boy-oriented book utterly lacking in psychology or spirit!"

I'd known she didn't like my book, or the intensity I brought to my book, but she'd never articulated my doings in such a heartless way.

"Escapist?" I said. "You know what, Adrianna? F-U-C-K you."

"Now, now," my mother quavered. "Don't start . . . spelling."

" . . . I've seen those index cards scattered around the house. I don't understand the point. Are you writing a diary? An account of your adventures? A 'captain's log'? Why are some of them written in silver, and some of them written in purple? They seem like the ravings of a lunatic. I found one in the bathroom the other day."

She sprang up and ran out of the room.

"Where is she going?" my father asked.

I knew where she was going; I also knew how to take advantage of her absence.

"Adrianna is having a hideous sick twisted love affair with an older man who you know and trust!" I blurted.

Adrianna ran back into the room, squinting, holding one of my cards in her clumsy hand. She began to read aloud its contents in an extravagantly objectionable tone.

"'Well, let 'em come, lad, let 'em come. I've still a shot in my locker, which is how he turns the Black Spot around. Always time left to turn fate around—'"

"An affair with who?" my mother broke in.

"What?" The blood drained from Adrianna's face. She realized she should never have left the room. Not for a minute! Fetching evidence against me, my ass!

"Don't you want to see this card?" Adrianna faltered.

"No, I want to know about you having an affair. Is he married? Is it someone we know?"

Adrianna looked stricken. I don't know why she thought she could trust me. With pleasure my mind leaped ahead to the long ugly scene that was unfolding, the slow torturous way my parents would extract the mineral details from her granite psyche. But in fact, there was hardly time to relish the event. Adrianna was actually dying to unburden herself. No sooner had the question been asked than she collapsed in a heap and began telling my mother all about it. She seemed pretty oblivious to how much she was upsetting my mother in the telling. "Oh, he's wonderful, Mom," she said as she put her head into my mother's lap and began to weep. "But it's tearing me apart. All the secrecy and lies. It's better that you know about us. You won't be angry with him, will you? Promise me you won't be angry, Daddy. Daddy?"

She turned to my father, who—rare event—had been listening. He was also biting his spoon.

"Who is it?" my father said.

"Don," Adrianna said with a shivery, hopeful smile. "Your colleague, Don Tatum."

My father stared stunned for a moment. He picked up his

bowl and threw it against the electric range; it shattered instantly and fell in pieces onto the floor.

"What?" Adrianna said.

My mother pushed Adrianna's head out of her lap and began to cry.

CHAPTER 19

One of the reasons I kept index cards on *Treasure Island*—not that anybody in my family deserves to know—is that I was devising a system to cut like a machete through the book's dense undergrowth. At the top of each index card, it was my habit to write a quotation, which encapsulated an important *lesson*. Beneath this line, in my own words, and in as succinct a sentence as possible, I wrote the lesson's *distillation*; and beneath this, in a smaller hand, one or two notes about the lesson's practical *application*. For instance, card #12 contained these helpful words from Jim Hawkins: "I began to be horribly frightened, but I kept my head, for all that." So below that the lesson: "Keep your head, even when you're scared or you think things are going haywire." And then under that, I wrote my application: [but this part I always wrote in code in case the card should come into the wrong hands].

"How many of those damn cards do you have anyway?" Adrianna asked me. It was one in the morning, of the same night in which The Affair Had Been Revealed, and we were just getting around to sweeping up the pieces of the broken applesauce bowl. My mother, with uncharacteristic neglect, had abandoned the kitchen, and my father had followed her into their bedroom and then into the garage, where they had been yelling and/or weeping for three hours straight.

I crouched with the dustpan; Adrianna swept.

"A hundred cards," I said. "More or less."

"And they're all about *Treasure Island*?"

"Well, obviously."

"I read a few. What's a gunwale?"

I had forgotten.

"What are rollers?"

"I don't know!"

"Well, it's your book. Don't get mad at me!"

"What do you think they're screaming about?"

"I don't know. I left Don three messages."

"It's one in the morning."

"I know," she said, looking distraught. "Either he heard them and refused to pick up, or he went to bed early and hasn't got them. He goes to bed at eight thirty sometimes."

"I'm sure he does," I said. And then, as an afterthought, I added, "Well, I'm sure he'll call in the morning then." I was shocked by my niceness.

We dumped the shards of the bowl into the trash and Adrianna went off to bed, looking like a zombie. Later she told me she had slept with her laptop on her stomach, in case Don got her messages and decided to email. But silent was the Don. About 2 A.M. my mother emerged from the garage and staggered past me, where I sat waiting at the breakfast bar, and began to wash her hands furiously. She looked like Lady Macbeth doing the sleepwalking scene, only she had the advantage of anti-bacterial soap.

"Mom?"

She jumped. "Oh. You. What?"

"Um . . . where's Dad?"

"He wants to sleep tonight in the car."

"Oh. Okay."

There was a rather long pause during which I tried to decide if I should pretend that this was normal, or ingratiate myself to my mother by inquiring, more deeply, as to why.

I decided to skip it.

"And why are you up?" She put out a hand and absent-mindedly smoothed my hair behind my ear.

"Mom, a person has quiet and harmless but also personally helpful obsessions, and they're not to be trifled with just because a stray card lands in the bathroom. Honestly. I was surprised you let Adrianna talk so disrespectfully to me tonight."

"I'm not sure I'm following you. You're upset about the index cards?"

"I was sitting up waiting for you and I started stewing. I hope you don't believe Adrianna that I'm keeping a logbook. And the diary idea especially offends me. I would never stoop so low as to measure my life by the pulse of domestic time! Where's the mastery in it?"

"Hobbies are nice, dear. Never mind what anyone thinks about it."

"It's not a hobby! And why is Dad sleeping in the car?" The question just popped out; I swear on Israel Hands' watery grave that I didn't really want to know her answer.

My mother settled in beside me at the breakfast bar. "I suppose there's no point in having secrets now. Don Tatum and I have a bit of a history, you see. Which of course you and Adrianna have no way of knowing about. It was when you and Ade were very small. Your father was just starting out at Leonard Milkins, and Don was the new assistant vice principal. There's a long version and a short version. But at this hour, I think a short version will suffice."

Which is how my mother came to tell me, quite abruptly, that twenty years earlier she and Don Tatum had, for a period of three weeks, fallen into a passionate affair while my father taught summer school, and that she had mistakenly ascribed more importance to the sex act than it warranted, and temporarily left my father, only to return, six days later, asking for forgiveness. Which, she added judiciously, had been granted, so far as it was possible with these things.

"You *left* Dad? Where was me? Where was I and Ade?"

"You were with your father."

"But you said he was teaching summer school. Where was we—where were we—during the day?"

"Maybe you weren't with your father. I think Aunt Boothie might have come to stay. You should ask your father. It was only a week. It's a long time in a young marriage, but a very short time in the span of a life."

"I can't believe you are minimizing this. You had sex and because you liked it, you *left* us?"

"It wasn't the end of the world, it was just an adventure." My mother smiled. She seemed to be enjoying her memories a little too much, forgetting that the essential note to strike was one of repentance. "It was . . . We were . . . Oh, it's just too complicated for my brain right now," she murmured. "We'll all deal better with this in the morning." She stood up briskly. "I'm glad you're mature enough to handle it. Thanks for listening. Nighty-night."

She tripped off to her bed, her neat little figure disappearing into the darkness of the hallway.

Had I heard her right? Had she called *that* an adventure?

This was a woman who lived in a world in which nothing dangerous or exciting could be undertaken; a woman who devoted herself to the tedious, net-mending tasks of family life. She had subscribed to *Bon Appetit* for three decades and still had every issue, arranged in chronological order. How could *she* have had a restless heart?

An abyss of possibilities opened up before me. Now would be an excellent time to attach my mouth to a cask of cognac, but my parents didn't keep hard liquor. I dug up the original hand-lettered sign I'd made on a creamy seventy-pound piece of paper with a lovely deckled edge—

BOLDNESS
RESOLUTION
INDEPENDENCE
HORN-BLOWING

—and stared at its sharp-tipped letters. If my mother embodied the Core Values better than I did, I would never forgive her.

CHAPTER 20

I don't think I slept a wink that night. In the morning, when I heard the others in the kitchen, clanking around with their coffee cups, I crept in. I could hardly believe we were going to eat breakfast together, knowing what we all now knew. Except, I realized, as I saw Adrianna drizzling syrup on her frozen waffles, *she* didn't know it yet.

"You're up early," my mother said to me from her position at the sink. The coffee maker gave a shudder and began to hiss.

"Didn't want to miss the part where you divvy up the spoils and the blood money. Where's Dad?"

"He decided to take his coffee and toast in the car."

"He went to work already?" Adrianna asked absently.

"No," my mother clarified. "He just wanted to eat in the car."

"You're kidding." I opened up the kitchen door, which led directly into the garage; there sat the Taurus, and in the Taurus sat Dad, with the windows all rolled up, staring straight ahead, slurping his coffee. He had a view of the rakes and the half-empty paint cans. I closed the door.

"If he's going to sit in the car," I said, "why doesn't he at least park it in the drive and enjoy the daylight?"

"Maybe he likes the gloom," Adrianna said.

"He can't handle anything," I said.

"It's the quiet."

"If he wants *quiet*, he could have breakfast in the dining room."

"Or in his study."

"Or in a box."

"Stop it!" my mother cried. "I WON'T HAVE YOU TWO CRIT-ICIZING YOUR FATHER!" She dropped her dishtowel and left the room.

Adrianna sighed and squeezed the plastic syrup bottle until it sighed and wheezed with her. "*I* didn't say anything! Jeez, what is going *on* with everybody? I know they're upset about me and Don, but come on; we're adults; we have a right to pursue consensual sexual relationships."

I sat down beside her and studied her graceless attack on the waffles. The house seemed extraordinarily quiet, and the counter, which had not been thoroughly cleaned last night, was scabbed with applesauce. My mother was melting down in her bedroom; my father had traded the house for his car. "Those useless parents," I said. "They have left me to tell you."

"Tell me what?" Adrianna said.

I tried to say it gently, but in my enthusiasm, I blurted out the tale more coarsely than I planned.

"Mom did *not*," Adrianna said. "You're so incredibly sick. You've always been jealous!"

After fifteen minutes, in which I had to hold both her wrists to stop her from hitting me, she went from outright denial to an imaginative reworking of the facts. Maybe Mom had had a crush on Don, and Dad had been jealous. Maybe there had been a kiss, at most—a quaintly romantic kiss in the very distant past. I begged her to believe me; about our own mother I would never have thought to invent, let alone burnish, these facts.

"She fucked him, Adrianna. Ask Don, or better yet, ask Mom."

I dragged her to our parents' bedroom door, which was closed tight. From inside we heard the awful high sound of our mother weeping.

*

For the next few days our family freaked out in a quiet way. My father went to work, but when he came home, he pulled the car into the garage and stayed there. Adrianna, who parked her car in the driveway, went to work after he had left, and continued to sleep in the house, but avoided all contact with my mother. My mother, normally in constant motion, managed to appear convincingly as a slow-moving version of herself. She continued to cook dinners, to which only she and I sat down. In order not to talk about what was happening, we stared out the window at the crust of snow on the lawn or else talked— and this was the surprisingly nice part—about *Treasure Island*. For long stretches she would be silent, pulling abstractedly at her hair, and then she might suddenly refocus on me, and ask careful, light questions about "my project."

"So is it an essay you're writing? Or as Adrianna said, a log book?"

"No and no. I don't even know what a log book is."

"A log book's where the captain writes down all the daily information he needs to keep the ship in order. Things like the ship's coordinates. And how the wind is blowing. Fuel and provisions. Who's on crew and what sort of maintenance is going on."

"Okay, I get the idea."

"Barometer and visibility," she said, perking up. "Temperature and tides. The state of the sea. Squall warnings."

"All right." I tried to shut her up with a wave of my hand.

"Continuous advance of the boat, distance, ground speed, sea state, waves, wind force and direction, clouds . . . "

"All right already! Enough already about the clouds!"

There was a terrible silence—it reminded me of the wedding when Aunt Boothie's wrap-a-round skirt fell off on the dance floor and everyone froze, even the band stopped playing.

"Your father hates me," she said. "All of you hate me for something I did twenty years ago."

"We don't hate you," I muttered. "It's just . . . we don't want to hear about it."

Earlier I'd found her sprawled on her bed with a satin box of mementos from her sole adventure. "Come here, look at this," she said, refusing to see how her souvenirs embarrassed me. "My hair was so dark then!" "This is a photo of your father and Don Tatum, playing table tennis. You should have seen how hard Don returned the ball. He had to change the rubber on his paddle every week!" It was as if she had no shame.

"Maybe Adrianna hates you," I said, "but I'm sure she'll get over it. He's her first boyfriend, you know."

My mother clucked dismissively. "What about Eddie Wisbey? That nice red-headed boy from . . . "

"They never went out. I forbade it."

"You're so *hard* on your sister. She wasn't terribly attached, was she? I mean, I know he's a nice man. And very sensual. Probably more available emotionally now that he's matured."

"Mom, stop! I *cannot* hear this kind of information."

"I'm sorry."

" . . . easier to fight you with a cutlass than hear this kind of talk."

"I thought you liked candor."

"I like *my* candor. There's a big fat difference."

"There certainly is. Do you want any dessert?"

I shook my head.

In the days immediately following my mother's revelation, I began to feel just a bit more like Jim Hawkins. Not the Jim Hawkins I had long admired—the boy who sails off to seek treasure, and upon discovering the crew is a murderous gang of pirates, grabs a gun and heads east to the shoreline, careless, clear-headed, and brave. I was more like the Jim Hawkins when absolute blackness settles on the island, and adrift in a coracle, he is unable to pinpoint the position of the anchored ship.

My mother and I continued to have dinner and she continued to release little pieces of information about her affair with Don Tatum. Often this information acted like a time-release capsule in that, when she shared it, I didn't immediately feel its impact. She might ramble on, impressed with my maturity, and I might nod, feeling somewhat interested, neutral, or, I thought, inured; but before an hour passed I would be reeling from the unwanted information, clutching my head and feeling dry-mouthed, about to vomit. To make matters worse, Adrianna seemed to intuit that my mother was confiding in me. She and Don were on the rocks—I didn't know the details, but figured she was giving him a hard time about having concealed the maternal history—and every morning, before she went to work, she barged into my room, her breath reeking of coffee and Listerine, and knelt over my bed, hissing at me to tell her everything Mom had said. "I don't know anything, I don't know anything," I'd murmur and try to fall back asleep. One morning she got so angry she pelted me with stuffed animals before she left.

The lowest moment came at half past eleven on the fifth night. Distraught, I had gone to bed early, and was tangled in a thick woolly sleep when there came a knock on the door. When I didn't answer it, my father came in. He was bleary-eyed and wearing his pajamas. It seemed frighteningly intimate.

My father has never done anything remotely sexually inappropriate—I find it hard to believe my father has ever done anything remotely sexual—but I have seen a lot of TV movies about incest, so I pulled the blankets up to my chin.

"I need to talk," he said.

"Keep indoors, men," says the Captain when Long John Silver humps up to the stockade waving his white flag. *"Ten to one this is a trick."*

"Talk about what?"

My father looked so stricken at this question that I decided to rip out the heart of my remark and hand it to him, bloody and throbbing, because in some ways here was the man-to-man talk I'd been reading in *Treasure Island* and wanting.

"Dad, I don't have the slightest desire to talk to you. Whatever's going on in this house is between you and Mom and Adrianna."

He leaned against the door. "It's a family matter. You're a part of this family. Let me come in a minute. I've been sitting in the car six hours straight and my back is killing me."

"Whose fault is that? If you had any communication skills you wouldn't need to sit in the Taurus. I don't even believe in your despair. Anybody who was really upset would gas themselves, right? But you're just sulking, waiting for someone to ask you how you're feeling. It's passive aggressive, Dad. Just go make up with Mom."

This little whiff of temper seemed to both surprise and animate him. He stepped into my room and closed the door behind him.

"I don't need to make it up to your mother. She's the one who should be making it up to me." He drooped as though he might sink to the carpet. Were those tears in his eyes? God no. "I'm so confused . . . "

That was enough. I leaped out of bed and steered him out the door. "Back to the car, Dad. Or wherever you want to be right now. I don't care where you go, but you certainly can't start having a relationship with me *now.*"

"Is your sister all right?" he whimpered.

"She's a mess, but isn't she always?"

As soon as he had left—I listened to make sure his footsteps returned to the garage—I let out a howl of fear and indignation. Then I got on the phone and called Patty Pacholewski. She didn't pick up, but I was frantic and left several messages. In the first I said only "call me back," in the second I intimated that there was "a bit of a crisis," and in the third I apologized outright for how pushy I was and begged her and Sabrina to let me move into their spare room, pronto. After the final message, which was quite protracted, in that it contained a lot of subordinate clauses and parenthetical phrases, and ended on a falsely jaunty directive to "call me back, okay?" a depression fell upon me like a ten-ton anchor.

I tried to sleep but my father's lost, wet expression kept coming back to me. For twenty years the man had had *no expression,* as far as I could remember. Where did he get off having feelings now?

When the phone rang I fell upon it.

"Patty," I said.

Richard awoke from the noise and stirred under his cover.

"This is Sabrina. The apartment thing isn't going to work out."

"If it's about the bird—"

"It's not about the *bird.* He's great and all, but Patty and I decided. Not interested."

"But if it's a matter of rent—"

"We never promised you anything. You had your chance, it didn't work out."

"But the parrot, he's not—"

"I said, it's not about the bird, it's about *you,* all right?"

She hung up.

I stared at the phone. "It's not over," I vowed.

"It's big, it's hot, it's back!" Richard said.

In bed that night, my mind was a storm: thoughts, like sea birds, hung screaming and circling in the air. Occasionally a bird landed on the cliff, took a shit, and wheeled off. I tossed and writhed and kicked the sheets into a twist.

Admitting defeat I snapped on the light. In my desk drawer I had twelve yellow Xanax hidden in an amber bottle. With the heel of a stapler, I hammered them into a powder. Half out of my mind I went to the bathroom and lifted a handful of aspirin, three of my sister's allergy pills, one Ativan, and two codeine left over from my father's root canal. These I added to my powder and then I went into the kitchen and prepared a stovetop box of macaroni and cheese. Seven minutes and the pharmaceutical mixture had blended beautifully into the neon grit of orange cheese sauce. I imagined scarfing the lethal dish and being discovered, with a great wailing, by my family as the watery winter morning light spilled across my bed. I took the saucepan into my room and flung the cover off of Richard's cage.

"Eat!" I urged like a Jewish grandmother.

Reader, I felt sadness while he ate it, but I love macaroni and cheese, and this batch was all for him. An hour later he looked much the same, though he was hanging upside down from his perch. "It's big, it's hot, it's back!" he said in a fruity voice, then bit the bars of his cage and said, too joyously, "Scraaww!"

"That's the last scraw," I answered, for his spirit—still buoyant under the weight of pharmaceuticals—maddened me. Would I never be rid of him? Oddly, a phrase from an old report card tumbled back into my mind: no ability to learn. He was a sick bird. From under my bed I took an enormous opaque plastic bag from T.J.Maxx, wrapped it around his cage and tied it tightly with a ribbed stocking. Through the plastic I saw him haul himself heavily from side to side and peck at the barrier, but he weakened before he could pierce a single air hole. He fanned his tail, swayed from side to side, gave one last angry call, and then lay down and let his soul return to its Maker.

When I was sure he was no longer breathing, I shucked off the stocking and the bag and lugged the caged corpse into the bathroom. Then I returned to my room. I felt both faint and terrified. I must confess that at this point, it wasn't the bird's sufferings that distressed me, but the idea that his spirit might come back, twisted and bitter and bobbing like Shirley Temple. I ate the remaining macaroni and slid into a nervous twitchy sleep.

In the morning, my mother came into my room, without knocking, and opened the shade. When she was convinced I was alert, she sat on the side of the bed and took her hands in mine.

"I have some bad news."

"I'm lying down."

At first I feared I would have to make a spectacle of myself—cry out in disbelief, wrench my hair, do *something* to simulate shock and grief—but my mother didn't seem in the least mistrustful, and received my (admittedly flat) "Are you sure? Are you kidding?" without suspicions. Perhaps she herself was too broken up by Richard's death to register the peculiarities of my reaction. Together we went into the bathroom to view the body, and I made some feeble excuses as to why he hadn't slept in my room the night before. (He'd seemed fussy and I thought he was hot, so I'd moved him.) My mother admired his plumage, murmuring in a reverent tone about the greens and the yellows and the white rings around his eyes, and I acknowledged that it had been hard to take in his full beauty when he was so alive and mobile. Still standing in the bathroom we discussed the formalities of burial, which I thought best to defer, in case I wanted to go back to the pet store and demand a refund. Does a Yellow-naped Amazon come with a money-back guarantee? my mother asked.

"Don't know," I said, but it was hard not to feel the allure of eight hundred dollars in cold hard parrot-green cash. More to the point, I was dying to take a shower—"and I'd like to be in here alone," I said—so I asked my mother to bag the body and put it in the freezer. Would she refuse me? My pulse accelerated, but in no time at all, she lifted Richard's body out of the cage and sealed it in a Ziploc ten-gallon double-zipper Big Bag.

"We have to tell Adrianna," my mother said as she closed the freezer.

"We do?"

"Before she goes to school." She washed her hands, dried them on a twisted dishtowel. "It would be wrong to let her go off not knowing. Before you shower, I'll make you some breakfast. What would you like?"

"Nothing, really."

"Grief is a wound that needs attention in order to heal. We can have pancakes."

Nobody rises to the occasion like my mother. She brought out the mixing bowls, the spatula, and the fry pan. Her pancakes became a bit of solemn pageantry, the stately measuring broken up only occasionally by anxious glances at me. I know she expected tears. She gave me a short hug after she cracked the eggs. "I'm fine," I said, pushing her off. When Adrianna's step was heard in the hallway, she threw down her wooden spoon and ran off to intercept her.

"Adrianna, look at me, sweetie. Never mind the other thing for a moment. I have news."

"Is something wrong?" Adrianna tipped her head as she fastened an earring.

"Yes."

"Is it Dad?"

"It's Richard. He's dead."

"No, he's not," Adrianna said evenly. "I just heard him."

"Impossible," my mother said, startled.

"You didn't," I told her.

"Of course, I did. I always hear him when I'm getting dressed."

"But not today. What did he say?" I asked sharply.

"He squawked. He did his beak-grinding thing—"

"I don't believe in ghosts." *Avaunt! and quit my sight! let the earth hide thee!* "Obviously she heard something else. Right, Mom? He's been dead all morning."

My mother solemnly opened the freezer.

"Oh no," Adrianna said. "Dickie Bird!"

"Sit down and have some pancakes," my mother said, resuming her position at the stove. It was clear to me now, my mother possessed the pragmatism of a true adventurer.

CHAPTER 21

We didn't have pets as kids. Nobody from prom died in a prom car accident. I didn't go to camp, so nobody from camp drowned in a lake. My mother's parents died before I was born, and my father's parents are still rotting away like apples in some nursing home in Nebraska. I only met them once and can barely remember it. So I was surprised at how complicated it felt to lose somebody. I felt relieved, of course—my room was my own again—but I also felt regret. A touch of disgust. Rage. Confusion. And sweet grief, which I'd never known. Yes, under the hard peanut brittle of my anger at Richard, which, now that he was gone, was fast dissolving, lay a pudding-soft layer of sadness.

"He's dead. What does it matter that he couldn't say, 'Take that, and stand by for trouble'? He's dead."

My mother was clearing the table. "Death does give you a different perspective, doesn't it? It shows you just how trivial some—" But here she picked up the butter dish, and seeing that someone had cut into the butter with a crumb-laden knife, she frowned, and began to shave away the grubby end with a fork.

Richard's death was a convenience for me, but soon I discovered that his death was a convenience for everyone—a bucket to put under the ceiling's leaky patch. We were upset; he was dead; now we had a respectable reason for being upset. Much easier to speak of the bird with exaggerated affection than to speak of what was going on between Adrianna and

Don Tatum (he appeared to be avoiding Ade's calls), or Don Tatum and my mother (she appeared to be fending off his calls) or my father and Don Tatum (Mr. Tatum's tires had been slashed in the school parking lot, and although nobody could prove my father's involvement, a Taurus was rumored to have been seen speeding crazily away from the crime scene). It was definitely easier to speak of the bird than to speak of what was going on between my mother and my father (still living in their separate spheres and not talking, although I did find a Post-it note on the breakfast bar that said *Prunelax*, which showed that however big the rift between my parents had been, it had not grown so wide that my mother was disbarred from buying his dietary supplements). Meanwhile Richard's body remained untended inside the freezer. I should go, I thought; I should go to Cutwater Pets and demand my refund; and yet I avoided him completely, and drank my drinks warm. A week passed.

My mother began to complain. "He was important, I know, but I really miss the freezer space." She left a brochure on my pillow called *Pet Bereavement: When Only the Love Remains*.

One day I pulled open the door and, past the ice cube trays, stacked up high like a cemetery wall, I saw him there—a little hoary with frost, but visibly Richard, recumbent on three bags of edamame. His eye, that damnable parrot eye, was frozen wide open. *J'accuse!*

My first impulse was to fling the Big Bag onto the snow bank under the kitchen sink window; my second impulse was to lie to my mother about why I had left the window open; my third impulse was to get her off my back and just bury him. But the idea of digging his grave in the frozen earth was unthinkable. I hadn't been raised for hard labor.

Should I call Lars? I could impress him with my aloofness—"I thought you deserved to know"—and inquire respectfully if he wanted to take care of Baby's remains. But he might say no, or he might say something about him and Rena.

No, only one person could be drafted for the job and that was the person who did all the chores in the family that nobody else wanted to do, the particularly unpleasant ones, such as unclogging the toilets and putting in the window-unit air conditioners.

Unfortunately I hadn't exchanged a word with him since the night I'd ejected him from my room. And my mother wasn't about to trot out to the garage and put in the request.

"Dad?" I knocked on the driver's side window. He had cranked back the seat and had fallen asleep in there, reading the newspaper, which had now, thankfully, settled over most of his face.

He startled awake and turned the ignition on, just for a moment, so he could depress the window.

"Do you want to come in?" he asked and began to fuss— clearing papers off the passenger seat, tossing an orange peel onto a dirty plate.

"That's okay. I'll stay out here."

As quickly, and as humbly as possibly, I explained to him my request. I guess nobody had told him that Richard was dead, so there was an inefficient, almost embarrassing, bit of backtracking to do, but he listened hard and seriously, and only when I was done did he sigh and drum his fingers on the dashboard. "Can't anyone else do it?"

"You're the strongest, Dad."

"What about your mother? She's no kitten."

"She has a lot on her plate right now."

He looked at me intently. "Did she *tell* you to ask me?"

"What do you mean?"

"Does she *want* me to do it? Did she *authorize* me to join the family in this capacity?"

I'm not sure when the family had become so bureaucratic, but clearly he needed to feel that my mother had engineered my presence here, that I was in fact her flunky.

"Ain't too proud to beg, Dad. She *wants* you to dig the hole and to be a part of the funeral. You know what she's like."

"All right," he said, pulling himself together. "I'll do it. Are they ready? Let's not waste time. Let's do it now."

And that is how we came to bury Richard—or rather how my father came to bury him while my mother and I watched through the kitchen window, making cheese straws.

"Cheddar or Parmesan?"

"Why not both?" I answered. "And can we open the Merlot?"

"I wish your sister would join us. No, not that Merlot. Here, I have a nicer one." She took out two wine glasses, then on second thought, two more. "Will you ask her? She would feel terrible later . . . "

So far the occasion felt both melancholy and snug: the oven's warmth, my mother's classical music station, the chipping sound of my father's shovel. The ground was not frozen, but hard enough that my father satisfied himself with a shallow grave, a choice he regretted a few days later when we saw the neighbor's German Shepherd, Audrey, trotting the boundary line with a feathery green bundle in her jaws. At that moment, however, the interment seemed just right. I didn't really want to include Adrianna, but at my mother's urging, I went and knocked on her door.

"What?" Her muffled voice emanated pain and self-involvement.

I pushed open the door. She was sitting on her bed, looking raddled and sad, cradling her phone and a box of Kleenex.

"Do you want to come to Richard's funeral?"

"I just got off the phone with Don. He's dumping me."

"The old man is dumping *you*? Does that fool honestly think he can do better?"

My surprise gratified her.

"It's that business with Mom. He doesn't want to cope with

it. He doesn't want to process my feelings. I love him, I'm sure if he would just *listen* to me, we could get past it. It was years ago! But of course, I'm angry and confused, and rather than *deal* with that, he's just running."

"What an asshole." Men really had very few emotional skills. "Come on." I returned the phone and the Kleenex to the nightstand and pulled her out of the bed. "You'll feel better if you come. Get your mind off him. Besides you belong with your family at a time like this."

In the kitchen I was surprised to discover my father at the sink, washing his hands. My mother stood a few feet away, writing in ball-point pen on the back of a napkin. It appeared that they might have passed a few civil words.

"Oh good," my mother said, turning.

Adrianna didn't meet her eye, but my mother's strategy was to let the formalities of a service carry us through the awkwardness. She poured the wine, distributed glasses, and invited everyone to take a cheese straw while she spoke.

"We're gathered here today to mark the untimely loss of our family's pet, whose name was Richard."

"Little Richard," I added.

"All right," my mother said, annoyed to be interrupted. "I've written a poem in his honor. Please forgive the roughness of the meter." Every facial feature rippling with self-satisfaction, my mother began to read the tribute she had just "dashed off," only a portion of which I give here.

> Dry his water dish, bag his carrots,
> Our Richard is dead, our king of the parrots.

Beware the occasional poet who has lacked an occasion. Out of my eyeshot she had dashed off a sonnet, a villanelle, and a sestina. We had seconds on our wine before she had come to the pantoum.

"Which, just to remind us, consists of a series of quatrains rhyming ABAB in which the first and the third lines of a quatrain recur as the—"

"No," my father put in, "the second and fourth lines recur as the first and third lines of the succeeding quatrain. Each quatrain introduces a new second line."

"You're right, darling. It's ABAB, BCBC, CDCD. Right? I *think* I did it right."

"Shall I have a look?"

My mother hesitated, then moved aside so that my father could see. They bent over the napkin together, my father murmuring, my mother inclining her head ever so gently so that her forehead rested against his ear. "Yes. Oh yes. Lovely! You have it. And the closing quatrain rhymes ZAZA."

They looked at each other without intensity, but with affection. I was both relieved and deeply embarrassed, as if I had stumbled upon the primal scene. Then my mother read the pantoum with my father still beside her. "Anybody want to add anything?" she asked when it was done, looking round.

Nobody did. Adrianna began to cry, tears dripping sloppily down her face.

"Did you love him?" my mother said sympathetically.

"Yes!" Adrianna blubbered.

There was a long interval during which Adrianna wept quietly, then raucously, then quietly again, reminding me of the ungainly crescendos of the coffeemaker.

"I miss him," Adrianna said hoarsely.

"Of course you do. So do I."

"I love him," Adrianna croaked.

"Yes, yes," my mother cooed. "So did I."

"Are you guys talking about the parrot or about Mr. Tatum?" I said, upon which my mother's tender expression disintegrated, and the softness in my father's face congealed, quite suddenly, like yolk on a plate.

After the funeral my father returned to the house. Things between him and my mother still seemed strained, but he slept in their bed and he came to dinner. After a while Adrianna too began to attend dinners, but didn't make much social effort. Being dumped by Don had obviously hit her hard. She looked angry and disheveled and moony all at the same time. "What's the matter?" I said a few times. "What do you *think's* the matter?" she replied haughtily.

If she didn't want to confide in me, that was fine. I had my own wounds to lick. After thinking it over many times, I decided, despite the obvious awkwardness, to talk to Patty Pacholewski about what had happened. I figured that if I could see her apart from Sabrina, I could make her understand that you can't judge a person by her bird.

I left the house well after noon so that I would miss the lunch rush, and yet when I sloped into the sandwich shop, there was an unpleasant line in which I had to wait, unsure of whether Patty even knew I was there. When at last I inched up to the counter, she said hello grimly, adding nothing other than what her job required.

"Was that sandwich for here, or to go?"

"To go," I said, a trifle testily. (I had said so beforehand.) With an impersonal thrust she removed my sandwich from the red polypropylene basket and dropped it into a grease-proof bag. Never mind that I had revered her for all of fifth grade, she nudged the bag across the counter as if she didn't give a shit.

I bit the inside of my cheek to staunch my tears. I had planned to tell her that Richard had died. I had planned to say, "If the only thing standing between us as roommates is that embarrassing bird, it might interest you to know that the embarrassment is now biodegrading in the yard." But instead I flushed bright red and fled from the shop.

At home, my mother was unloading the dishwasher in her introspective way, giving every glass and plate a solemn inspection. I sat down at the breakfast bar, unwrapped my sandwich and made a terrible discovery.

"Not a single red pepper! It's a grilled chicken and red pepper sandwich, and look, Mom, there's nothing but chicken inside."

"There's some peppers in the fridge."

"*Roasted?*"

She made an insufficient clucking noise. Oh, Saturdays, infernal Saturdays, a wilderness of snares! Before I could say anything more, my father came in and began to fling himself noisily about looking for his car keys, and as soon as I saw he meant to enlist me in his petty search, I plumped my sandwich onto a plate and fled to the living room, where Adrianna had decamped on the sofa with a mess of library books. She looked up moodily. I settled myself in the armchair and observed that she was combing through *All About Parrots*.

"Why're you reading that?"

"No reason," she said. "Just curious."

"Mulling over the past's not healthy. You're not thinking of getting another parrot, are you?"

"No, mostly I'm just wondering why he died. He wasn't all that old, you know."

I cast about for something plausible. "But he was . . . very negative. That might have hurt him in the long run."

Adrianna sharpened her gaze. "Did you know birds should never be fed avocado, parsley, chocolate, or caffeine?"

I yawned. "How about a grilled chicken and red pepper sandwich with *no* grilled peppers?"

"And no peanuts either. Didn't you used to give him salted peanuts as a treat?"

She began to read aloud from an Optimum Diet chapter in

a classroom-specific drone, the custom of lecturing to captive children having eroded her God-given ability to assess a listener's interest. "Onions, no," she said. "Butter, no. Salty foods, no. Dairy . . . "

"He's dead and buried. Horrors!" I said, pulling open my sandwich for further study. "This chicken was taken off the grill too soon. What is she doing, trying to give me salmonella?"

"Dairy, no. I distinctly remember cottage cheese. Tabbouli. Avocado chunks and even some bite-size Snickers. You couldn't have fed Richard worse if you'd tried."

"It was Mom who liked to treat him." With thumb and reluctant finger, I picked up a book on the floor, *Natural Healing for Parrots,* and quickly threw it down again. "Why are you reading all this? It's a moot point." I handed her my plate. "Would you taste this please and tell me if you think it's underdone? Do you think it's an insult, this sandwich?"

"It's not good, but it's cooked."

"Aha! So no *intentional* harm." I left the sandwich in her hands and went off to my room, satisfied that although Patty hadn't yet forgiven me, she wasn't aiming to kill me. But my sister, in her nest of books, hadn't been gathering grass and twigs as light entertainment. She had a hunch. And while I took a late afternoon nap—the sleep of the innocent, the sleep of the slightly depressed—she rolled that hunch between her fingers until it grew into a thing of prodigious proportions. For years I have insisted that, despite her serviceable academic track record, Adrianna is not (warning: confidential family information) *all that bright.* Dogged, she is; organized, yes; pedantic, check; but possessed of a signal, sinuous, investigatory mind?

Ha! Ha! Ha!

And so it seemed incredible, in the highest sense of the word, that such an uninspired person should discover, in her imagination's underbrush, the secret I had marooned on my desert island heart.

CHAPTER 22

A few nights later when I was sitting at my desk, reading my book, Adrianna knocked: rat-a-tat-tat-BANG (four light knuckle swats, one lead fist).

"Enter," I said with superb indifference.

Enter she did, rather wildly, tumbling through the door, her face aflame, her eyes lit up with madness. In her hands she held the T.J.Maxx bag—that oversized, unforgettably useful bag. I should have thrown it away—a murderer always throws away the weapon!—but knowing my mother's fondness for recycling, I had put it in the pantry.

"I think we should talk," Adrianna said.

"Can it wait till morning?"

"No, it can't."

"If this is about Mr. Tatum, I'll tell you everything I know."

That diverted her for a moment. "This isn't about Don," she faltered. "But why—what do you know?"

"I know he and Mom have been talking."

It was true that I had caught wind of some phone calls, but that had been days ago, when the news first broke, and even then I didn't know for sure what my mother or Mr. Tatum had said. Only that he had been calling her.

"Sit down," I advised. "I didn't want to worry you, but the fact is, it's been worrying me. Do you think—oh, it's too humiliating to even say it—do you think there's any chance of Mom and Mr. Tatum getting back together?"

I watched the idea of their union bloom in the great arid

desert of her head like a time-lapse video of a blooming cactus. She must have changed color three times as she contemplated it. Then she laughed—her unattractive hyena laugh—and shook it off.

"You're crazy," she said. "There's nothing going on there. That was just a dalliance in their past."

"Sure it was, but who knows? If Mom isn't satisfied with Dad—which, how could she be?—maybe your thing with Mr. Tatum wakened her old desires for him. And maybe his contact with *you* wakened his desires for the woman who got away. You know, there's nothing like The One Who Got Away!"

"You're vile."

"I'm imaginative," I admitted. "But it could be happening, without us knowing it, and just think! Your affair with Mr. Tatum might've been the spark that started it."

She sneered and shook the plastic bag at me. "You know why I'm here, don't you?" she said in a low voice.

"I *don't* know, Adrianna. I just assumed . . . "

"Don't play games. You hated your bird from the beginning and you neglected him for his whole sorry existence. You fed him toxic foods, you cramped him in the cage, you never so much as bought him a jingle toy. But when he hung on—and what a fighter!—you wised up and decided to do the dirty work yourself. Directly."

"Adrianna, what are you talking about? Stop the Angela Lansbury business at once."

Her face shone. "That bird didn't die from natural causes, and you know it. There are feathers inside this bag. And feather dust. Smell it!"

I guided the bag away from my nose, marveling at the shelf life of that fetid odor. "You poor thing," I said, switching tactics. "Stop rattling the bag and calm yourself a second. Animals die every day, remember? Think of the spiders we squash in the bathtub. The ants we used to burn with magnifying glasses.

I know what you're going through with Mr. Tatum—well, actually, I can't *imagine* how I'd feel if I found out Mom was banging Lars, but I *do* know what it means to have your heart broken. All the same, let's not get animal rightsy. If I'd allowed myself to get mushy every time a frog expired at The Pet Library, I wouldn't have had the energy to keep living. You have to just swash through it all. Sensitivity is a peril. And you know what Jim Hawkins would say? He'd say what good is a life if it can't be dashingly used, cheerfully hazarded?"

"That book again." Adrianna stared at me, aghast. "Listen, a parrot doesn't get to make choices like you; it doesn't get to play pirates. Torn from the wild, a parrot depends on you for its very existence."

What a pathetic pile of scrupulosity, what a lot of quibbling!

"I was BOLD, Adrianna. I'm a fool, if you like, and certainly I did a foolish, over-bold act, but I was determined to do it."

"So you admit it? You admit you used this retail bag to suffocate your own parrot?"

"I admit nothing."

Shuddering, the bag crackling in her hand, Adrianna walked out.

CHAPTER 23

In *Treasure Island* the pirates send a note called the Black Spot when they intend to throw you out of the gang. We used to pass notes like that in elementary school, only usually we didn't draw anything as clear and direct as a Black Spot; it was more verbal—for example, once we wrote a girl named Etta Statchnik a note titled: Everything Wrong with Your Ears and Your Clothes and Your Hair. After that we penned a long list with categories and sub-categories. As I say, it was no Black Spot, but it tipped her off that she was no longer welcome to sit at our lunch table.

One evening not long after my scene from *Murder, She Wrote,* my mother said that the next day she would need me out of the house. She was going to do some major cleaning. "Why can't I stay in my room?" I said. "Because," my mother said crossly, "I'm cleaning it *all.*" She arranged that Adrianna would drop me off at a mall near St. Catherine's School for Girls, and in the afternoon, when Adrianna finished teaching, I could take the bus to school, and Adrianna would drive me home. It was an odd plan, but my mother gave me nearly a hundred dollars of pocket money and squeezed my arm. "Treat yourself," she said. So I went with it.

At the mall, it is possible to amuse oneself without effort. I tried on sixteen party dresses and asked the sales assistant to hold five. For lunch I ate a quinoa salad with a plastic fork while sitting on a bench by the Trevi fountain. Then I trolled the jewelry counters and shoe racks. After dropping eighty dollars on a tub of body butter, I ran for the bus.

Half an hour later when I deboarded in front of St. Catherine's School for Girls, I realized that my hand was too light. I'd left the swanky bag of body butter on my seat, but the bus lumbered on, its tires making two black lines on the snowy white road. Too bad. Streaming towards me on the pavement, came a clutch of girls, pale and drab, their slate blue skirts hanging beneath the hems of their puffy coats. I dodged their wheeling bodies and pulled open the school's heavy door.

The hallway was overheated. Too much glitter, too much glue, I thought as I passed the bulletin boards, cluttered with holiday art. Inside Adrianna's classroom, my sister stood with her back to me, erasing equations from the blackboard.

"So this is where you go every day," I marveled, having never thought much about her work life, except to mock it in a general way.

"Let's get out of here." She looked hot and sweaty as she chucked books and papers carelessly into a filthy canvas tote.

"Actually, I'm curious about your set-up," I said, ambling down an aisle, examining the desks' innards. Crayons, markers, pencil boxes, glue sticks. I flipped through a spiral. "Are you *really* marking this girl down because she made bubble letters? Check minus? And she dotted her *i*'s with hearts!"

"Put that back and let's go. Mom is expecting us at exactly four-thirty."

"Mom's not going anywhere. She's probably still vacuuming."

"Yes, but the others . . . "

"What others?"

When she tried to backtrack, I pretended to believe her story, partly to see what dumb thing she would say next.

"No others. I mean, just Mom and Dad. We're going to have pie with Mom and Dad. Mom called me. She made a cherry and cheese pie. Isn't that your favorite?"

"Yes." I gave her a fake smile.

"Good. Then let's get out of here."

In the hallway she paused to find her keys. Then she decided not to lock her classroom; the janitor would clean it. No, she decided, she would lock it after all; the janitor had a key. I watched her sweaty hands fumble with the lock.

"Adrianna," I said after a careful pause, "you're not still smarting about Richard's death, are you?"

"I'm not. Looking back over everything, I realize that whatever happened between you and Richard, you were seriously mixed up when it happened." She glanced warily at me to see how I was taking her interpretation; was the sauce too rich? was the seasoning right? "Don't take this wrong, but I think you may be struggling with a kind of addiction."

"I don't take drugs, Adrianna." I banished the memory of Richard's final meal, which we had shared.

"No," she said slowly, as if humoring one of her third graders. "But you do have trouble distinguishing *your* reality from whatever happens on Skeleton Island, right?"

"Not exactly," I said, but she took my arm and ushered me through the hallway, telling me softly to never mind, nodding to various homely colleagues, pressing my arm, and gently guiding me into her car. By the time I was in the passenger seat, belted in, I had begun to feel oddly sedated. She wound my scarf around my neck and said a few yum-yums about my mother's cherry and cheese pie. I wondered aloud if we needed to stop on the way home and get a pint of vanilla ice cream. Then I caught myself.

"Now, look you here, Adrianna," I said, staring unseeing through the windshield as the car bounced along. "I am not such a fool that I don't see what you're up to."

"I'm taking you home, where we're going to have a nice piece of pie."

"Yeah, but why?"

"What do you mean, why? Why . . . pie as opposed to cake? Do I need to explain that Mom's done the apple cake way too many times?"

"It smacks me as a little suspicious, me being shucked out of the house all day and now you rushing me off for an appointment with pastry. Did you know Mom gave me spending money today? A lot of it!"

"You're making a big deal out of nothing. Mom cleaned the house. And then she wanted to bake. Is that so hard to believe? She baked a pie and she asked me to hurry us home so we could eat it."

"Us and who else?"

"Okay. Friends," she admitted after a little sulk. "People who know and care about you."

"I can't believe you!"

I scoffed all the way to the house, which turned out to be about fifty yards, since we were already at the bottom of the drive. Adrianna parked her car, as usual, under a small stand of pines, lumpy with snow. When I opened my car door, the air was leaden.

CHAPTER 24

They were in the living room, seated in a semi-circle across from two empty armchairs. They had teacups in their hands and folded papers in their laps. The overhead lights were off, and the table lamps emitted a feeble pink glow, so in the late afternoon light the expressions on their faces weren't clear. But they were identifiable. They were my mother, my father, Rena, Lars, and my old boss from The Pet Library, Nancy Wang.

They said hello and remained seated. Rena smiled at me and waggled her fingers. Adrianna sat down in one of the empty chairs and gravely thanked them all for coming.

"This is a joke," I said, stomping about behind her. "I know what you're trying to do, and you're not even doing it *right*. An intervention is supposed to have a special counselor. Where's the professional?" Right away, they had been cheap.

"Listen, I know all *about* intervention," Adrianna drawled. "I read about it on the web."

"And it's supposed to be a gathering of people who are important to me, people for whom I have the greatest affection and respect, who would have the greatest impact on my life if I lost them. So what the hell is *she* doing here?" I pointed at Nancy.

"I know you are an addict," Nancy said loudly.

"Still smarting about Willie's haircut?" I rolled my eyes. "And where is Beverly Flowers? Where is my healer?"

"I asked her," Adrianna said sulkily. "But she said she had to pay a parking ticket."

"Please sit down, darling," my mother said. "We're all here because we care about you. Come sit down. Would you like a glass of water or a cup of tea? We have some things we want to share with you."

I dropped myself into the empty armchair and surveyed them. While I had been standing, I'd been afraid to look at Lars as if, by not looking, I could prevent him from looking at *me*. Not that I still cared for him, but an ex-boyfriend always induces the question: Do I look good enough to inspire major regret? Seated, I saw that he looked a little jumpy, his hair was tousled in a sweet way, and he was staring at me, without blinking. He appeared fascinated, almost excited. Everyone, in fact, seemed pretty keyed up, except for Rena, who sat with her hands in her lap looking dispiritedly at her vegan shoes.

Adrianna began officiously. "We think you have an addiction to a book, and we think it's led you to make some pretty poor choices. Choices that have been causing yourself and lots of other people pain." Here I said I had to go to the bathroom, but Adrianna said, "Look, we've all worked very hard on this, so please don't interrupt."

"Darling, isn't she allowed to go to the bathroom?" my mother asked. "I thought you said this wasn't going to be an attack."

"Yes, I'm just saying let us get *through* it, okay?"

It now became apparent to me that Adrianna was sweating profusely; where other sweaty people have half-moons under her arms, she had dwarf planets. She turned to me: "Everybody here can bear witness to the ways in which your obsession with that book has led to the damage of yourself and others—"

"Five fish gone!" Nancy shouted as if no time had passed and she and I were still standing in the puddles of The Pet Library. "Rooster eat dog food! He very sick!"

"Don't worry, Ms. Wang, everyone gets a turn," Adrianna said. "We've each prepared a list of things that we'll no longer tolerate, finance, or participate in unless you give up this *Treasure Island* nonsense—"

"It's not nonsense. Not one of you has even read it, so none of you knows what you're talking about."

Lars smiled a little. "*Yo-ho-ho and a bottle of rum!*"

"*Shiver me timbers!*" my mother tittered.

"*A smack of the sea about him!*" hooted Adrianna.

"*I did a foolish, over-bold act, but I was determined to do it!*" said Rena.

"*By thunder!*" said my father. "*By the powers!*"

"Five fish gone!" Nancy shouted above the derisive laughing.

"All right, so you don't like the book's style. That's your business. But I know my rights and I'm not hurting anyone by being inspired by a piece of nineteenth-century literature."

People exchanged looks. My parents shifted uncomfortably in their chairs. Rena bit the callus on her thumb, and Lars pulled off his glasses and rubbed his eyes. Adrianna was enjoying herself now, you could tell.

"Who would like to start?" she said primly. "Rena?"

"Oh, no. Maybe someone in the family?"

"I'll go," said Nancy.

"We heard from you already," I said.

"Don't you dare be rude to Ms. Wang," Adrianna said.

"Would anyone like some more tea?" my mother asked hurriedly.

"I wasn't being rude. I was being BOLD."

"And now she's HORN-BLOWING," Lars said gaily, looking round at the others for recognition.

"You're certainly feeling your oats!" I cried. "Why are you even here, Lars? It's over between us. You can't threaten me with a list of things you're no longer going to finance or tolerate because you're no longer in my life!"

Everyone gasped; even I was surprised at how cruel I sounded. And yet what was my mean streak if not the flavor shot in Lars's coffee? The equanimity with which he met my bad temper convinced me, even now, that my surliness was necessary to his comfort. It enlivened his blandness.

"I know I'm not in your life. But you and I were together long enough that I thought you'd forgive my intrusion here. I came out of duty and affection; your sister said you'd gone off the deep end, and that if we didn't band together and help you, who knew what would happen next."

"What melodrama! You can *look* at me, Lars, and see I'm not off the deep end." I smoothed my hair, which I could feel had gone a little haywire, and wiped the spit from the corner of my mouth. Whenever I shout, I expectorate.

"I see"—and here he gave me a look of such quiet, unqualified admiration that my hands fell from my hair.

I don't claim to know everything about deep and long-lasting relationships, but I can tell when a guy is crawling into the palm of my hand.

"You're not off the deep end," he said. "Maybe you're teetering on the edge, but aren't you always? Still, if I could be of any help . . . "

"Lars, I always liked you," my mother said, reaching across the semi-circle to pat Lars on the thigh. Adrianna flinched. I could see the whole train of horrid associations in her face, but I wasn't threatened; my mother wasn't the least bit his type.

"I think this is becoming just a little too much of a free-for-all," Adrianna said. "What about the lists?"

"Can I just say one thing first? Before we move on?" Rena turned eagerly to me. "I noticed you giving me the evil eye before, and I thought maybe I should explain, that the little possibility that we last discussed on the phone—"

"Out with it, Rena," I grumbled.

"Well, it's a private matter."

"There are no private matters in this house, Rena," said Adrianna.

"Oh. Well, then, perhaps I had just better clarify by saying"—and here she lowered her voice—"Lars and I are not, as you might have thought, an item." She explained that they had gone out once, fought bitterly about whether eating less meat could affect climate change, and decided the only reason they were even seeing each other was because—hurrah!—they both missed me.

As I let this revelation soak in, it seemed as if my ivy-covered castle had just been visited by a pesticidal genius whose application of the proper chemicals had made the heavy green curtain over my windows shrivel; in brief, the sun shone in.

"Did you kiss?"

"No," Rena said. "We never even touched hands."

Thank god, I thought, looking at Lars and remembering the way, despite all the complications between us, our mouths had tended to meet in perfect harmony, relaying a tenderness our speaking selves never managed. Should we have kissed more and talked less?

"Can we please get on to more pressing matters?" Adrianna huffed. "By now we should be well into the family's testimony about how you are ruining us with your obsession with *Treasure Island*. Dad?" She glanced at my father, whose eyes were dimming with sleep.

"Never mind. Mom? Let's hear from you first."

My mother picked up the piece of paper in her lap and unfolded it as if it were somebody else's dirty handkerchief. "*I refuse to keep enabling you and I will not sit here in pain and watch you*—Adrianna, what's this word? Oh, destroy–*watch you destroy your health and well-being*. Well, is that clear? Would anyone like some tea?"

"Thanks," I said when she went off to the kitchen. "That was very heartfelt."

My father, roused at last, leaned forward. "I have a feeling you're not taking this very seriously."

"Why should I?" I snorted. "I appreciate the attention, but I'm not about to give up *Treasure Island*. That book taught me more about how to live than any human being in this room!"

"Ouch," Lars said in his amiable way.

"This is terrible thing to say!" Nancy moaned. "Where is respect for mother and father? For family?"

My mother returned bearing a tray of tea things: pot, plates, forks, and a large pecan pumpkin pie.

"So much for cherry and cheese," I muttered to Adrianna. "Lies, lies, lies!"

"Get a sharp knife," my father muttered, as my mother stooped over the coffee table trying to serve. Between her distracted manner, the thickness of the piecrust, and the uselessness of her spatula, she was helpless before the pecan layer.

"You'll never do it with that dull thing."

"But she doesn't want that," Adrianna said when my father had fetched a six-inch knife, "that's for boning chicken."

My mother passed him the pie, and he cut wedges for everyone, destroying Adrianna with his efficiency.

"Is there going to be ice cream with this?" I said.

"No," Adrianna said crossly.

"If people ate less chicken," Rena observed, "the reduction of greenhouse gases would be something along the lines of 1.5 tons of carbon dioxide a year."

"Okay, then let's go on," I said. While they had been rattling around about the pie, I'd taken a moment to formulate my position. "You're all thinking I'm in a bad way: no job, no apartment, no boyfriend, no plans, my whole future gone to wreck, but do you want to know what? I don't care because *I* did it! After a lifetime of drifting and not-deciding anything, I *found* the book, I *made* the plan, and yes, I bungled up my job—but only because I no longer valued it. As for the parrot, it was I who found him, and I who took him to Lars, and when Lars and I weren't working out, you know what? *I* broke that up too!"

"Not to get technical, but I broke up with you," Lars said.

"Not now, Lars." My speech was roughly modeled on the one Jim Hawkins gives in the enemy's camp, and I was extremely pleased to realize I knew so much of it by heart. "I've had the top of this business from the first," I went on. "You can do your inexplicable intervention or you can leave me alone, but I no more fear you than I fear a fly."

"You do fear flies," Adrianna said blandly. "You're always asking me to go after them."

"Jesus!" I threw down my fork. "Just bluebottles, and will everybody stop interrupting?"

"But I want a turn to speak too," Lars said. "Adrianna said to write down what we—" He fumbled with the paper and stood up, bumping the table with his shin and rattling the teacups. "I've had a lot of time to think, you know." He emitted a convulsive nervous cough and then bore down on his piece of paper (graph paper, green tint). "When we first broke up, I felt as though you had sort of taken a dump on our relationship—excuse my French—but then I thought a while and realized it was more complicated."

"I should hope so," I interrupted. "God, why did I waste all that time with—"

"And I thought a lot about the beginning, when we first fell in love. The burritos. The hanging out. We never tried to fix each other, we enjoyed each other. Then you met the book and developed a new attitude, and although I admire you for striving, even when it seems you don't know what exactly you're striving for, I don't think you had to go through all that. To be a good person I mean. I think you were already fine; the more I think about it, I know you were fine. So when Adrianna asked if I would come and help you drop the book, I said yes, but I did it with a secret motive. Actually, after you left, I got into therapy"—here his neck began to effloresce in red patches—"and I figured out that you were right: I *had* been lying to my mother, and now that I can talk more openly to her—about a few things—it's better. Which I wanted to tell you and say thanks. So, I don't want to say you have to give up the book, because that would be—well, kind of hypocritical, and also, frankly, condescending."

"Lars," Adrianna broke in. "This is a total breach of trust."

"But if you do decide, on your own to give it up, and want to go back to an emotionally supportive kind of relationship, well, you know where I live. I changed the locks, but I could make you a key."

"This is good boy," Nancy said. She was smiling despite a mouth full of pie.

"Jeez, now what?" Adrianna rolled her eyes. "Are you going to propose to her?"

Lars coughed uneasily. "No. I thought—I mean, I'm trying to say—I miss you is all."

I missed him too, though who can trace the arc of an emotion in its entirety? I wanted him to miss me and he was a great kisser, but as Adrianna had snarkily pointed out: if he loved me, cough up the ring!

All this time Rena had been sitting very still, not eating her pie, her eyes half-closed in thought. I don't think she was really taking in the tentative steps Lars and I were making towards reconciliation.

"Listen," she said to me, "probably all of us knew that you hated your job and that you had some ambivalence about Lars. Also it's no secret that the way you read your book is somewhat partial. My nephew showed me the Disney version. 'Oh my god,' I said, 'this is completely different! How come she never talks about the *pirate* business?' But my concern isn't literary accuracy; it's Richard. I don't know what happened to him. And that's why I came today: to learn the truth about the bird."

"He's dead," my father said.

"*Who's* dead?" Lars said.

"I know he's dead," Rena said, "but did she kill him?"

I stamped up the crumbs on my plate with a damp thumb. "Rena has a soft spot for birds, and I know the rest of you thought of Richard as family. Well, he was as much a part of the family as Aunt Boothie's ex-husband—not the one who worked in the steel industry, but the one who ran off with his secretary to Peru, who Mom always suspected wiped his butt on the towel at Thanksgiving. I forget if he was Boothie's Two or Three."

"Did you hear the question?" Adrianna said.

My mother put down her teacup. "I know it's a sensitive question, but you can see, it *does* make a difference to us, if Richard died of natural causes, than if you, let's say, under the influence of a book, or whatever else you might be, unknown to us, downloading from the Internet . . . "

"Focus," Adrianna said. "Let her answer the question."

"Why on earth is everybody scrutinizing *my* obsessions? Don't you think other people in this family have damaging enthusiasms? Should we call up Don Tatum and let *him* have a word? It's not *my* book—it's *his* penis that ought to be getting an intervention!"

"Now you've gone too far," Adrianna said.

"I still can't get over it," Lars said, after a pause. His voice was listless and he twisted his napkin. "Nobody even told me Richard was dead."

My mother covered her head with her hands. "All right, we are not going to delve into these subjects again. This kind of conversation is destructive for everybody. Instead we're going to enjoy the pie. Tell me, Ms. Wang, do you think the nutmeg overwhelms the pumpkin?"

Adrianna was livid. "Do you want me go fetch that plastic bag? The one from T.J.Maxx that reeks of feather dust? Because this isn't about Don and me, or Don and Mom, or you and me, it's about whether you *took a life*." Her chin shook as she spoke. Fine rhetoric, I granted her that. But no matter how many arguments Adrianna made—and clearly she wanted to argue until she was blue in the face—I was not going to get exercised about my so-called shortage of PET-LOVE and SLOPPY KINDNESS.

"If you want my ear, talk about BOLDNESS, RESOLUTION, INDEPENDENCE, and HORN-BLOWING!"

"But you're none of those things!" Adrianna said. "Where did this boy-hero stuff come from? We had the same childhood! We shared an Easy-Bake Oven and a Lite-Brite, remember? You showed me how to use a tampon! We used to *like* the same books. Remember *Little Women?*"

"Is that what you think?" I sat up in my chair. "That we shared a childhood? We were two separate people in one house, treated differently, according to how *they* perceived our abilities and talents."

Adrianna rolled her eyes. "It's either Mom or Dad or me—anyone but you—who's to blame for all the stuff you don't like. You want to pretend Latin I and Latin II set me up for success? All right, go ahead and think it! But at some point you'll see your life is the result of your own sorry choices!"

I made a strange, guttural noise of exasperation, picked up the pie knife, and hacked at the crust on my plate. Butter crust, crumble shards. "That parrot died of natural causes and you all know it," I said. "And even if he didn't, you can't pin me with murder. If anything, it was a mercy kill."

"Mercy?" Rena said.

"He hated his life. A bird is supposed to be able to talk, and he couldn't talk—not in a meaningful way—and it made him really miserable. Plus, you know—he lived in a cage."

There was an appalled silence.

"I was an idiot to think we could help you," Adrianna said slowly. "I embody your values more than you do. It was bold of *us* to gather here, it was resolute. I wouldn't call us "independent," but so what? Interdependent people are nicer. You live like you're the only person in the room!"

"You studied my index cards more than you let on. I suppose now you're going to tell me you know more than I do about HORN-BLOWING?"

"Would you put the knife down now?" my mother asked me anxiously. "You're mangling that pie."

"Let her mangle it, Mom," Adrianna mocked. The intervention appeared to have robbed her of whatever stability she still possessed, for she repeated the statement hotly: "Let her mangle it! I'm getting sad for you now, I really am," she told me, a lowering shadow over her face. "You get inspired by stories about sailing the high seas, but you're like a dead goldfish, floating belly-up in the tank. It's pathetic! Ever since you read the damn book, you've been gearing up to *do* something, right? Well, *do something*, sister! Take a risk! Go somewhere! Get a job! Try loving somebody—for real, I mean, not just house-playing! There are all kinds of ways to have a life, but you're the only person I know who thinks she's risking something when she gets out of bed and thinks, do I have toast or cereal? Cereal somebody else paid for! You know what?" She was raving now, wheeling about the room like a crazy person. "I could *forgive* your passivity, if you were a gentle, deluded, slacker kind of person. But I can't forgive a deluded, slacker person who fucks with my relationship and kills an innocent bird!"

I jumped up only to speak, but seeing me lunge, Adrianna panicked. In a deplorable display of cowardice, she scuttled away from me and pressed her back to the wall. I could tell by the workings of her face, and the girlish octave of her screams, that she thought I was going to stab her. The thought amazed me—and in my newfound confidence, stab her I did, pinning her hand against the wall, causing her to bleed copiously all over the Thomas Kinkade print we'd gotten my mother for her fiftieth birthday ("a cottage radiant with the light of love seems to bathe all of nature in an atmosphere of breathless serenity").

Adrianna, did I do something at last?

I think I did. It was some time before I could remove the knife, partly out of squeamishness, and partly out of a sincere wish not to damage any nerve endings.

CHAPTER 25

Hours have passed since the intervention. Who intervened with whom, you might well ask. Who indeed. Yes, who. But now I am a little deflated and the pen is heavy in my hands. Regrettably I no longer feel like stabbing anyone.

I think I can skip over the particulars of the clean-up—predictable as they are. Adrianna bled against the Kinkade for a good five minutes, during which time Rena dry-heaved into a napkin and Lars called 9-1-1. At last, my parents wrapped the hand in a bath towel and hustled Adrianna off to the Emergency Room. The others fled, Nancy taking care to haul off the remainder of the pie. Alone in the house, I dropped into the chair where Lars had recently sat, and fancied I could smell his personal scent—something I'd always registered as a cross between Pears soap and tree resin. My hand, where I had gripped the knife, throbbed. The intervention had stirred feelings in me that I had been working hard not to feel these past few months. I was like a giant soup pot that had been left a long time to simmer on the stove, and now someone had come along and pried, with a wooden spoon, the burnt bits of onion and garlic, maybe even glutinous pasta, off the bottom. Those little crusty bits of food now floated to the top of the soup and they were, I believed, my feelings about Lars. Did I love him?

I called his cell and, after the preliminary greetings (hi, how are you, is your sister able to move her hand), I asked him if he'd meant what he'd said.

"Um, which time?" he asked.

"About how you missed me and want to make me a key to the apartment."

There was a pause. "Well, after seeing you go after Adrianna with that boning knife, I think maybe I underestimated the depth of our problems." Another pause, during which there rose, as if out of a deep trench, a stone wall that could not easily be breached. I had a flash of what I'd looked like with the knife in my hand—mentally speaking, an impressive piece of masonry.

"But when I *said* it, I meant it," Lars clarified. "I mean, I wouldn't have gone to all the trouble if I hadn't thought—but then, you know—you picked up the knife. And, well. It's probably my fault for being over-hasty in my fantasies about reconciliation. Because, um . . . things change."

"Do they?" I said ironically, although at that point I wasn't in full control of my faculties, and a little unsure of where the irony of the situation lay.

Soon after I hung up, my mother called from the St. Vincent emergency room to tell me she and Adrianna were walking through the entrance (I could hear the ppppphhhht of the pneumatic doors). My father was parking the car, she said; I wondered, aloud, if he would manage to come out of it. We hung up, and I rushed around the house in a pointless mania, washing teacups and plates, rearranging pillows. Ten minutes later my mother reported that my father had surfaced and that all three of them were waiting in triage. A kind nurse had given Adrianna something to staunch the blood. An hour later, she called again and said, "We're still in the emergency room. The delays are unconscionable." And then again at ten, she called, saying something incomprehensible about Adrianna's blood pressure. Most people can sustain a hand injury like hers without any trauma, so I ventured to wonder if Adrianna's complications had something to do with her excess weight.

"This is hardly the time to talk about *that*. Do you realize you may have cut the ulnar nerve?" My mother hung up.

By midnight, when they had not returned, I felt the need to propitiate the gods, so I took my calfskin bag and walked through the cold night air to the library, where, though I had marked it, bent it, and left thumbprints of garlic mayonnaise through most of Chapter XXIX, I returned the book to a weatherized steel book bin. It made a dull thud as it landed, scattering, no doubt, a bone pile of other books, whose titles and contents I'll never know. I felt a wild desire to stick my hand down the box's maw and grasp my treasure again, but I consoled myself by saying I could no longer be trusted with it. And that I could check it out again, if need be, when the library opened. Or buy my own copy, though of course it wouldn't be the same. No, no—scratch that!—I was done with the book. That was the point of the gesture: heal her hand! Plus, something else would come along one day and waft my consciousness higher.

At 2 A.M. my parents staggered into the house, looking grey and haggard. The TV had been blaring in their ears all night; they had eaten a lot of candy bars in the waiting room. Adrianna still hadn't seen a doctor and there was some concern about the ulnar or maybe it was the median nerve. I got the distinct feeling that my parents' patience with me had been exhausted. All these years in which I had refused to drive a car, all these months in which I had refused to get a job, they had indulged me without seeming to indulge me, but now they spoke to me with a flat expectancy in their voices that almost embarrassed me with its bare expression of confidence: as if I had been walking around naked all this time, and someone had casually handed me a towel.

"Take your father's keys," my mother said. "We told her you'd be there as soon as you could."

"Maybe I could take a cab?"

"You don't have cab fare."

"But I'm directionally clueless. I'll get lost."

"I'm going to draw you a map." My mother leaned over the breakfast bar, sketching quickly on a piece of pearl grey stationery. "This is our house, all right . . . You're going to go east on Curtis Boulevard . . . "

"She may not even want me there," I said.

"She's mad at you, all right. But she needs you. She's frightened out of her wits. She asked the triage nurse what was the worst-case scenario with a hand injury like hers."

"What did the nurse say?"

"It wasn't a rational question," my father said.

"The nurse said she didn't know what was the *worst*-case scenario, but she'd had a man in yesterday who severed his finger in a snow blower."

"Adrianna has a knife wound," my father said.

"—The nurse said sometimes you see a case where the hand doesn't get taken care of soon enough, so the nerves get compressed, and the hand just stiffens—" My mother stopped writing and held up one hand like a claw.

"Do you think she's going to *lose her hand*?" I asked.

"No," my father said firmly.

"No," my mother admitted, a little reluctantly. She was angrier with me than I'd realized. I didn't want to think about that.

I've never liked Long John Silver, but reading about him vigorously stumping around on his wooden leg prepared me to see the positive side of a crippled life. I shudder to think of it, but I know my strengths: I could lose a limb and, with the right wardrobe, still come off as sexy. I'm not saying I would *want* to wear a prosthetic hand, only that I'm the kind of girl who could pull it off, whereas Adrianna—what can I say? Her appeal is limited. Just as I was arriving at that conclusion, Adrianna rang. She sounded small and miserable. Was I coming, she wanted to know. Yes. What was I thinking about?

"Prosthetics," I answered truthfully.

She began to sob.

"Not for *you*," I hastily explained. But she was too far gone.

"Adrianna, come on. It's not like I did it on purpose. You provoked me, don't you think? Anyway, Mom and Dad said you're not going to lose your hand! You dialed the phone, right?"

"Fuck you!" she said. "You should be apologizing."

She hung up.

"Go brush your teeth," my mother said. "You can leave in five minutes."

I adjusted the driver's seat and the mirrors and took a moment to remind myself how to work the gear-shift (it was automatic, but still: it had been a while). Despite my sweating palms, I managed to inch my way to the driveway's end before I realized I didn't know whether to turn right or left. My cell rang. I put the Taurus into park and, as I answered, looked to the top of the drive where I saw my father's face pressed against the kitchen window, staring back.

"Drive," his voice came through the phone.

Sometimes I think all my problems stem from the simple fact that my parents never know when to back off.

"I'm going to," I said, and hung up.

I knew what the emergency waiting room of a metropolitan hospital would be like. Once when I was about ten, I'd gone with my mother after she had stepped on a nail while building a birdhouse. The place was like a bus station, with a dirty floor and aisles and aisles of vinyl chairs, bonded together as if in punishment. We'd waited an hour for my mother to get called for her tetanus shot. Seated near us were a man and a woman, neither obviously injured, both obviously insane, wearing matching running suits, and staring in front of them, without expression. There was also an old man who had fallen asleep and was drooling on his collar, and a few rows beyond him, a partially bald woman, her eyes bruised, her cheek bleeding. While we waited, a battered, foul-smelling man came in, half-naked, and screaming at the top of his lungs in a language I couldn't understand. Two men appeared and restrained him; I can't remember if he was led in or out. Children, my age and younger, cried, and whined, and slept on the chairs. The place smelled of urine, disinfectant, and fear. When it was all over, my mother had bought me a candy bar and said cheerfully, "Well, that's done!" as if she and I had just bought a fine bundle of corn at the farmers' market, and not languished for an hour in the company of human misery.

I steered the car carefully down the snow-laden street. It was dark, and there were no other cars on the road, but the birds were already making a racket. Their voices put me in mind of that other bird's voice, the one that ought to have said, "Steer the boat, girlfriend!" but more often said "boat" and "blowout sale" and "burger." Certain scraps of my story came back which I would rather not remember. Richard's eye, covered with freezer frost; Lars holding open the door that last time with a civil sadness; my mother's tartan wallet with gold leather trim from which I filched money while she showered; Rena saying gently, "Isn't it a boys' book?" before she picked up, for the hundredth time, the check; two ounces of eye cream I bought, owing to my naïve belief in the properties of seaweed extracts; a stipple of white fungus, untreated, on a beak; me standing in the living room, a truly helpless hamburger, unable to extract the pie knife from my weeping sister's flesh. Could a book like *Little Women* teach me what I needed to know?

I cracked open the window, and cold air pierced the warm reverie of self-incrimination. Don't think, just drive, I told myself, as I inched the salt-pocked car along the slush-ridden road. But I still didn't know which way I was going. I opened my calfskin bag and there was a map, as my mother had promised, in the pocket where *Treasure Island* had long resided—a neighborhood map, with compass, cross streets, library, shopping centers, gas stations, and every particular that would be needed to bring a phobic, geographically challenged driver to a safe anchorage upon St. Vincent's shores. I put the car into park and waited for the heat to kick in while I studied it. There was a big red X on the drawing of the hospital (which she'd rendered with surprisingly thoughtful detail, including cafeteria and parking). There was a star on our house next to which my mother had written: *You are Here.*

ACKNOWLEDGMENTS

Thanks of every coinage to my bold, but kind, agent Emily Forland, my sharp and fearless critic Jennifer Ruth, my early reader Janet Desaulniers, and my late and crucial reader James McManus. Moidores and sequins to Carol Anshaw. Doubloons and double guineas to Alice Sebold. A gold piece bored through the middle to wear around the neck to Chris Gaggero. And for Judith Pascoe, who sailed with me the whole way, the vast, uncountable heap.

Sara Levine's writing has appeared in *The Iowa Review*, *Nerve*, *Conjunctions*, *Necessary Fiction*, *Sonora Review*, and other magazines. She is the author of a collection of stories, *Short Dark Oracles* (Caketrain Press, 2011). *Treasure Island!!!* is her first novel.